MY CHILDREN HAVE FACES

MY CHILDREN HAVE FACES

CAROL
CAMPBELL

UMUZI

Published in 2013 by Umuzi
an imprint of Penguin Random House (Pty) Ltd
Company Reg No 1953/000441/07
Estuaries No 4, Oxbow Crescent, Century Avenue, Century City, 7441, South Africa
PO Box 1144, Cape Town, 8000, South Africa
umuzi@randomstruik.co.za
www.randomstruik.co.za

First edition, first printing 2013
First edition, second printing 2013
First edition, third printing 2014
First edition, fourth printing 2015
5 7 9 8 6 4

ISBN 978-1-4152-0183-1 (Print)
ISBN 978-1-4152-0498-6 (ePub)
ISBN 978-1-4152-0499-3 (PDF)

Cover design by Monique Oberholzer
Cover photography by Eric Miller
Text design by Fahiema Hallam
Set in Impressum

Printed and bound by Mega Digital, 6 Koets Street, Tygerberg Industrial Park,
Parow, South Africa

Ook beskikbaar in Afrikaans as *Karretjiemense*

For my mom and dad,
Winnie and Ron Graham

The Great Karoo

When Cold Winds Blow

Present Day

1 MISKIET

They move into my circle. When I open my eyes I feel a sparking, like electric wires in my head, and I know they are close. This time she is not going to get away.

No, Klein Muisie, now you are going to be sorry you ran away. You are going to be sorry you took my son.

For a while I keep my face on the same warm spot on the pillow, listening. I will hear them come. The donkeys will set the dogs barking when they get to the edge of the houses. They will have to pass my house to get to Leeu Gamka, so I lie, listening for the creak of the disselboom.

Ja, Klein Muisie, I have been waiting for you to come back.

Fifteen years watching the veld, knowing you are out there. You must be a dried-out old whore now. Running and hiding up and down the sand roads of the Great Karoo will suck the life out of a person. No, I am sure you are not a fresh, pretty girl with a clean doek holding a newborn in your arms. Now you are burnt black by the withering sun, your bones showing through your skin from hunger. It was a hard life you chose, Klein Muisie, and now you are coming back here, thinking I will have forgotten. You are coming back, thinking I have changed. Well no, a leopard doesn't change his spots. I have been waiting for you and nothing has changed.

There was blood on my pillow when I woke up. It had caked on my cheeks, and when I lifted my head I saw it was all over the sheets. The pain hit suddenly, in my mouth. During the night I bit my tongue. It was blood from my mouth that made this mess.

Today is the day, I feel it.

The dogs have started. Donkeys are coming.

I swing my legs out of bed and go to the basin to wash.

Today I will have my son and I will teach you a lesson. This boy will think his daddy is cool. New blue jeans, All Stars, Old Spice. No stink of unwashed bodies here. All these years of nothing to do but wait for you to come back.

I have had time, Klein Muisie, time to imagine my son's face, to think about the father-son things you stole from me.

Through the curtains I see the donkey karretjie pulling up the hill, Kapok cracking his sjambok. And there she is, sitting beside him.

I slip out the house and, from behind Ting-a-Ling's hokkie, I watch them come closer. A warm feeling pumps through my veins.

I knew all I had to do was wait. *You have come back, just like I knew you would.*

The boy is walking next to the karretjie. And, as if he knows I am here, he turns and looks into my eyes. I want to get out of sight but he is too quick so I look back at him and smile. We check each other out and then he turns away, never losing step with the donkeys.

Oh, Klein Muisie, I wanted you.

"Leave me alone."

"Give me a good reason. Always leave me alone. Why?"

"I am scared of you."

Were you afraid I would kill you too? But I wanted you too much.

You weren't scared. You wanted Jan, that was all. You thought he was a better bet. That he was a man with a job who bought you packets of chips and Fanta.

Well, it's too late now. Now the time has come to show the boy the truth, and I know that is why you've come back.

After the karretjie passes I follow to see where that old bastard Kapok will uitspan. He crosses the N1, steering the donkeys through a gap in the fence and calls a halt to make camp at the bottom of a bank near the road. Ja, Kapok was so quick to take Jan's place. My brother was only dead a few weeks and I was still making a plan when she went with him.

I go home and clean my bloodied bed then walk to the white people's church. The service has started. For the first time today the electric wires in my head stop sparking. As the Afrikaner women's voices sing hymns of suffering and long ago, my dream of last night comes back to

me. A dream of soft skin on a woman's shoulder breaking between my
teeth. Maybe that was when I bit my tongue.

2   MUIS

Since we left Leeu Gamka long ago I have moved like a dog on a chain.
One end of the chain is attached to a pole hammered into hard earth
and the other is rubbing my ankle raw. I make sure the chain never
goes loose, but the pulling has made me very tired.

I am not a dog and I cannot accept my chain is so short. I am thinking that if I don't break this chain, I am going to die.

Many times when I sat under a pepper tree or walked next to the
karretjie, I thought that to die from hunger or a snake bite would be
better than living like this. If Liewe Jesus could have chosen a time, I
would have been happy. I wanted my life to be over. But to die with the
devil's thick fingers around my throat is what made me sit all night
and watch the veld while everyone else slept.

We have come back to Leeu Gamka so we can eat. It's shearing
time on the farm Genade, and Baas Kobus sent a message for Kapok
to come. So many missed seasons, but Baas Kobus told Diksop to tell
Kapok he was wanted on Genade. Diksop is Kapok's sister and she
and Gawie, her man, live in a real house on a farm near Rietbron.
When Diksop found us we were at the uitspan at Seekoegat, and she
gave Kapok the message. I saw him straighten up and he smiled and
looked important and I knew we were going back.

When Kapok was a boy his family uitspanned at Leeu Gamka before moving on to the farms for shearing. While the shearers worked,
Baas Kobus, who was Klein Baas Kobus then, and Kapok ran together,
stoning koggelmanders and shooting mossies with their ketties.

Somewhere between it all, one learnt to be the baas and the other learnt to shear. Kapok could work eighty sheep a day when he was fed and healthy. Before he hurt his leg.

"My record is thirty-five before brekfes," he boasted to our children.

"Never, Pappie, we don't believe you."

"S'true. I will teach you one day, Fansie. Witpop, don't you believe your father is a strong man?"

Those thirty-five sheep before breakfast were sheared when Kapok was still named Joseph. Strong Joseph, before the donkey karretjie tipped and crushed his leg, leaving him to hobble like a chicken, a kapok. I wonder if Baas Kobus knows he is Kapok now.

I used to like farms like Genade. In the morning the women lit fires under the round, black, three-legged pots at the back door of the farmhouse and, before the sun was too hot, the smell of cooking afval and mieliepap would drive us all mad with hunger. The food was for the men. Meat helped their muscles, Kapok said. When it was dish-up time the girls spooned the food into their chipped enamel bowls and plastic tubs.

Some farmers didn't give the workers food. Most places we bought tins and flour from the farm shop and paid for them with sheared sheep. But on Genade the workers ate. If any of the food was left, the Klein Mies gave the girls bread to wipe out the gravy before they washed the pots and put them away for the next day's lunch. In the middle of the afternoon everyone lined up again for a cup of sweet tea. Kapok said that was his favourite time, when the tired men drank tea and smoked Boxer Tobacco and joked who was the fastest shearer and strongest man. At the beginning of the shearing season Kapok held his stomach in the night as cramps came in waves, sending him running into the veld.

"It is the milk in the tea, Muis," he said. "I am not used to it."

"You ate too much." I laughed.

"Maybe it's the water on the farm."

We both knew the cramps went away when he got used to eating every day. After the shearing time, the pain would come back but, this time, it would be from hunger.

What Kapok loved most about Genade was the Klein Mies. When the weather was hot she wore a yellow top and matching pants and a big hat to keep the sun off her pink skin. When she was outside she would put on dark glasses and laugh when the children ran away from her.

"She looks like a gogga with big black eyes," Kapok said.

"You mustn't be so dom, those are dark glasses to protect her blue eyes from the sun," I told him.

"If she doesn't wear them her eyes will turn black like ours and then she won't be so beautiful."

In the afternoon, when the work was done, Klein Mies called her girls into a ring and gave each one a needle and thread and showed us how to stitch lappies together to make blankets. I still have my needle and, when I can find a lappie, I stitch it on to my blanket that I have been making all these years. If Miskiet lets me live then I can show Klein Mies the blanket and maybe she will give me lappies.

Diksop said Klein Mies was like having a mamma all over again. "You can't walk around with that ringworm on your face," Klein Mies told Diksop. "Use this cream in the morning and evening."

She organised for the government nurse to come to the farm and all the women had to bend for a needle in the backside.

"You can't have babies all the time," the Klein Mies said. Diksop said her backside burnt for two days but she didn't complain.

"I let them prick my bum because I want Klein Mies to be happy," Diksop said.

Sometimes the workers drank a papsak at night, then their pappa, Baas Kobus, shouted at them the next morning.

"We know he is going to shout, but sometimes a person does things and only feels sorry about it afterwards," said Kapok.

"There is no time for drinking in shearing time. If you drink, you can go," Baas Kobus would shout. Hanging their heads in shame they went to work, the hung-over drinkers shearing only a handful and the women wishing for a regmaker instead of tea.

If the Klein Mies thought someone was too thin there would be a talk on eating vegetables and potatoes.

"Why do I see starvation on your face?" she asked me. "What's the story?"

She listened when I told her that my man was paid only R20 a day in some places and that he didn't find work very often.

"Sometimes we don't have food, Klein Mies."

Ag, Klein Mies, where does a woman living on a donkey karretjie in this wide dry land of jackals and scorpions find a bunch of carrots to cut into the pot with the creature she has killed for her children to eat?

"You mustn't spend all your money on wine and tobacco. That's why you go hungry."

"Yes, Klein Mies. You are right," I said.

I didn't want to come back. All these years this place has grown in my mind. The name Leeu Gamka makes my head deurmekaar and then I can't talk and I want to go into the veld with my children and hide.

"Anywhere in the Karoo but, I ask you, not Leeu Gamka, Kapok. We can go straight to Genade and pass Leeu Gamka."

"Muis, it's too far to the farm for the donkeys."

"He will kill me."

"We must leave the donkeys and the karretjie with my people."

"I will not get away from him again."

"He is older now and not worried about a dusty-faced piece of kai-ings like you."

But I know he hasn't forgotten. Blood he spilt soaked into the dust of this place while I watched.

"You had your chance to do this nicely."

We are in the tunnel under the highway. He has waited for me.

My mouth tastes sand and his weight comes down on my lungs. I close my eyes so I can't see him laughing.

14

Words form in my mouth but no sound comes.

Then I hear Jan's voice. "Muisie, wait. Muisie, wait for me. Have you got the Fanta I bought for you with my tips?"

Help me, Jan. Help me. Praying that the words in my mind will reach his ears.

Air and breath. Like a spider I crawl to the wall and try to stand.

Jan and his brother circle each other like two fighting dogs. Jan's shouting makes me open my eyes, but all I see is the quick, silver knife.

Each day of the long trek back to Leeu Gamka the chain loosens more. There is no choice. The veld is black from the sun. The watering holes we know are dry and, although no farmer ever turns us away from his water, many have none to give.

"Please Baas, can we water our donkeys?"

"Ja, but don't let them graze, there isn't enough for donkeys and sheep."

The donkeys drink deeply and when they wander off we catch them again and lead them back to the karretjie outside the farm gate and let them find what they can in the langkampe between the fence and the road.

But the langkampe grazing is gone and Pantoffel and her foal, Rinnik, have no strength to pull the karretjie very far. No matter which way we go there are fences protecting the sheep's grazing. The donkeys are so hungry that when I light the fire their brown eyes follow my hands as I stir the pot or knead bread.

When Fansie brings in a bony rabbit one night I dish a bowl for each of them and they eat it. Starving donkeys eat our meat, crunching bones between their teeth like two dogs. This has been the way, for the last weeks, that we keep them alive, until Kapok decides we have to move south, closer to the mountains.

"The cold winds are coming and the Swartberg brings more rain than this desert land. I know people who can help us there."

When Diksop finds us she is excited. "Baas Kobus and the Klein

Mies will feed you. They have been asking for Kapok every year for fifteen years. You must leave a message for them at the Ultra City at Leeu Gamka and they will come for you."

Now, as we steer the karretjie back towards Leeu Gamka, all these stories come back to me and I wonder, if I live another day, if I will see the Klein Mies again and sew lappies and have an injection in the backside.

The NG kerk's steeple grows taller as our donkeys struggle towards town.

The chain is going loose and I know the time is coming closer when the years of running like a rabbit will be over.

3 WITPOP

I stink. Really, s'true. When we come to town, the children hold their noses and poke me with sticks. If I try to hit them they run away laughing. So I spit. Like a snake. If I am fast then I hit them with my spit on the legs and that makes them mad and then they want to come back and hit me. The little ones and the other girls are scared of me so they throw stones. If I can spit in their faces then that makes me happy. But I don't laugh, I just curl my lips back like I am going to spit again and they run away screaming. I am not scared of the big boys. They can hit me and push me but I don't care. Nothing they do can hurt me on the inside, even if they kill me.

Last time in Prince Albert there was a big boy who looked nice. He was playing with the little children and being so kind. When he sat down I went and sat near him but he said, "Stinking karretjie girl, sies, get away from me. You stink."

I looked at him and felt juice in my mouth. Really, I was going to spit a big one and hit him on the nose but something made me stop.

You were playing nicely with the little kids, boy. You are ugly to me but I won't make you run away screaming.

I stood up and walked away and sat under the thorn trees and watched them. Some of the children looked dirty, just like me, but they didn't stink. They didn't like my veld stink. I don't go to school and I can't write my name. I also think children don't like that. If they ask me about writing then I lie.

"I can write it. My name is very long and I don't have time to write it now. Ssshhhaaarrrmmmaaayyynnn. That's my name. It's very long."

Some of the girls in Prince Albert have new clothes and hair with white ribbons in it. Really, how did their mammas get their hair to grow so long? I wanted to ask them if it was sore to have their hair pulled and twisted in vlegsels but I was too scared to go near them.

"Stinking karretjie girl. Voetsak!"

If the clean girls' mammas saw me walking too close they called their daughters. "Come in. She'll make you sick," they said. "Those people give you germs."

Germs. Is that the sores on my mouth? I don't know what germs are, but Fansie says they give you omlope that itch and make circles on your body. There's lots of circles on my body.

My hair is a bush that stands straight up like it is reaching for the sky. When we stop at a watering hole I look at my hair in the water and I wonder why it grows straight up like that, like grass. I don't think my hair can be put in vlegsels with white ribbons.

They have shoes, these town girls who hate me so much. Pappie says we don't need shoes because our feet are tough like dogs'. "Shoes are for children who go to school. Why do you need shoes?" he says. "You must be glad you don't go to school, children hate school."

Fansie and I laugh, and Pappie laughs and we forget about shoes. But sometimes I wonder. What would it be like, squeezing my toes in black school shoes?

The funny thing is, even when the town children hit me and run away from me I want to go to school with them more than anything in the whole world, but we never stay long enough for me to go. Mamma says we can't go because we don't have birth certificates.

"Birth certificates mean you are registered and then you can go to school. None of you are registered so that means no school. Now shuddup."

Karretjie people like us don't worry about papers. Papers are for white people and for coloureds who want to be white. S'true, Pappie said that. We are not white people, Pappie said, and we are not coloured people who want to be white. We are karretjie people and we are free.

"Where am I going to get you a birth certificate in the middle of the veld?" Mamma said when I asked if I can go to school.

We don't have birth certificates because Mamma doesn't have an identity book. She was never registered, so she can't register her children and we can't ever go to school. Really, it's a whole lot of can'ts. Mamma can't be registered because she was born at a moddergat with no one but her mommy and the moon to see her come into the world.

"The government wants a person to be born in a hospital before they will register you. How am I going to prove where I was born when I don't know the day or the year? I don't even know which moddergat it was where I popped out."

"Just make it up, Mamma," Fansie said.

"And if the government finds out? Hey? Then I go to jail."

Mamma just doesn't want us registered. She wants us to move with her and Pappie over the veld on the donkey karretjie and not go to school.

"If you go to school then I have to run around finding stokkies for our night-time fire and you all start getting big ideas," she skels me.

She says I already have big ideas, wanting school shoes all the time.

I ride on the karretjie and I think about school shoes and white

18

ribbons and writing my name. Maybe if I went to school my teacher would be a pretty juffrou with high heels and a car. I don't want an old cross man to be my teacher. I like pretty lady teachers who smile and give you lekkertjies.

You know what I think? I think Mamma doesn't want to have us registered because she wants us to be invisible and never be anywhere for long.

Really, I don't care what the town children say about me. They know nothing about the veld. Fansie says they would die if they were left alone out here.

"They just know 50c chips and green cooldrink," he says. "That stuff is rubbish, it makes your teeth green and your hair fall out."

Fansie also doesn't care about the town children, but when we get to Prince Albert he always disappears to find Oom Poenie who gives him a cigarette. If Oom Poenie's son from Vredendal is there then Fansie gets a drag on the Mandrax pipe. He likes that, he says it makes him feel really, really lekker. All I know is he lies on the ground like a dead snake, smiling at all of us for the rest of the night.

We are going to town. Not a big town like Prince Albert, but Leeu Gamka. It's a place with a school. Pappie said to me before we get there I must wash in the bucket and then the children will play with me. I won't do it. S'true, I like my smell and I won't wash in the bucket until they buy me a pink roll-on and a waslappie. I told him that too.

In Rietbron I do have one friend who lives in a house. She's Didi, my cousin. Her mamma and pappie have fixed jobs and Didi lives in a real house on the farm, with a TV. When we are in Rietbron I sleep on the floor by Didi's bed, but Fansie doesn't like it and he always comes to fetch me and hits my legs with a stick till I run to Mamma crying. But then she shouts, "What are you doing with those people?"

"I want to watch TV," I cry. "Really, I want to watch 7de Laan with Didi, please Mamma."

When I cry like that Mamma stops skelling and says I must come back to the karretjie and use my time to wash while we are near a tap.

But what's the point of rubbing sand under my arms and making it all mud with cold water? I want a pink roll-on and a lappie. Then I will wash.

So this time we are going to Leeu Gamka and I feel like it's different. We have never been here before and Mamma is very, very quiet. Maybe we can get birth certificates and go to school now. I am sure we can. That's why Mamma is so quiet.

She knows if we are in Leeu Gamka we can get her an identity and then we can get birth certificates and go to school.

"Pappie, can we get birth certificates in Leeu Gamka? If we do that then you can get an All Pay grant and buy food and," I whisper so only he can hear, "a doppie, Pappie."

"There is nowhere to get birth certificates in Leeu Gamke. We are going there so we can find a way to eat," he says, without smiling at me.

I can see he is thinking about All Pay and a doppie.

Mamma says nothing.

4   MUIS

I hear my children's names floating on the wind across the veld. They have no papers and they tell me this every day.

"Mamma, we have no papers."

"Mamma, we want to be registered."

Why are they so worried about this? Always, all they want is this piece of paper.

When we come near a town they start again. "Can we get papers in Rietbron?" Seekoegat, Prince Albert, Klaarstroom. Every town it's the same question.

They should be registered. I know that. Without government names, who will the police search for if they are lost? And, when they find them, how will they know they are mine?

That is why I tell Kapok we must keep away from the towns. Under the sun and the moon I can see they are mine and keep them safe. Fansie's darting eyes, Witpop's cheeky mouth and Sponsie's open arms are what I know. In the veld I can see them and keep them safe. From him.

If he finds us, the first one he will take is Fansie. When the police ask me: "Who is this Fansie?" I will have nothing to show that he is alive or that he is mine.

He wants my boy. Since before Fansie was born, he has wanted to take him for his own.

He looks at my tiny baby, his face like a male baboon with sharp teeth, seeing his own flesh and blood.

Leave him, he is not your child, I think, too scared to speak aloud. You are a murdering bastard.

Towns are not kind places to my children. I see Witpop trying to play but the children hit her with sticks and throw stones at her. Fansie disappears to smoke a Mandrax pipe and then lies useless in a corner. And me, when I see a town rising up from the veld, a thirst rushes in my blood for a doppie. Just a little wyntjie to let me forget my troubles. Then I can't stop myself and I have to get into town and find a one litre, quickly. Now we are in Leeu Gamka. It is the one place I never wanted to see again but we have trekked across the plains and we are here. The red houses on the hill are the same. The big road with the hissing and shouting trucks is the same. The Shell Ultra City is the same and, as we come over the hill, I see that the tunnel where Jan died is also the same.

There will be nowhere to hide here. In my mind I see the shiny flash of his knife. I want to shout to my children, "Run! Hide in the veld!" Small hands and feet must vanish behind a bush or a rock or down a hole. They know how to disappear because I have shown them.

When a farmer chases us off his land, three sets of little eyes watch, like duikers, ready to run. He thinks it's only me and Kapok and the donkeys. He does not see them in the aardvarkgat or behind a rock. I make sure then that they do not exist.

"Hide, hide," I whisper now.

"Mamma, we are in Leeu Gamka. We don't need to hide." Witpop is laughing at me. "Nee man, Mamma, really. We are in town. We don't have to hide here."

But he is here. Now, more than they have ever been, my children are in danger.

They are not registered. They don't exist.

Long ago, when Fansie was still very small, we went to the school in Seekoegat to ask if he could come to learn his letters and numbers but the principal wanted his birth certificate or his clinic card.

Straight away we hitched the karretjie and left. Where must I get a clinic card in the middle of the veld? Why can't they go to school and learn to read and write before we move on again? Always a birth certificate. Always a piece of government paper.

My daughters were born in the veld under the karretjie. When it was time, I cried out to the mothers and grandmothers of the old time for them to help me bring them into the world. When they came they were small and slippery and, every time, I thought I had given birth to a frog. Kapok cleared their mouths with his finger and, each time, he laid the baby under the blanket next to me.

"It's like a lamb," he told me, "sometimes you have to clean out the lamb's mouth and make sure it drinks."

He tied the cord with tou and then, when it was all over, he cut the baby free with his knife. We kept away from towns so that no word could go back to Leeu Gamka that Muis had daughters. He would want them too. I knew that.

My Fansie is born in a dark room on a mattress behind a thin curtain in the red brick house in Leeu Gamka. Jan is dead and Miskiet is sure he is my baby's father. He sits on the other side of the curtain at the kitchen table, smoking while I give birth to my boy, alone, with a lappie in my mouth to stop my screaming. Afterwards, when the baby is in my arms, he comes and looks at him.

"That is my son," he says and laughs and walks out of his house.

When I can, I stand up and wash his coffee mug and empty the chipped bowl of ash from his cigarettes. There are ten stompies in the bowl. I keep two, with a little tobacco left, for myself.

He doesn't touch the baby in the few weeks I stay in his house. All the time we are there he looks pleased. He leaves me alone, knowing there is nowhere I can go. My people are in Fraserburg and I need to be stronger if I am going to walk.

It is impossible to steal food from him, but every day I scrape a few tablespoons of flour into small pieces of newspaper and roll them in the bundle with my baby. If I am going to walk home to my mother I need food. This flour and the old Boesman ways my mother taught me will keep me alive.

My mind was filled with plans of escape and my mother when Kapok found me under the pepper tree. Fansie was a month old and I had started to tie him on my back to make him ready for the long journey. I had decided I would hide from the sun and Miskiet in the day and walk with the jackals and the moon at night.

"Mina is dead from the TB," Kapok said. "I need a woman to come with me on my donkey karretjie." I nodded. Mina had been sick for a long time.

"Come, and I will raise Jan's son like he is my own."

"When?"

"This malletjie says he is going to Beaufort West for three days next week," he said, nodding at Miskiet's house. "There are a lot of them going, to try for government road work. We will go the first night after he leaves, when it's dark."

I looked at him and nodded. Maybe Kapok would take me to my mother.

"Okay, I will get ready."

Now we have come back. Fansie is nearly a man. Many times I think that without him we would not eat. Kapok's stiff leg makes him too slow to catch anything, but Fansie runs all day with his dog, Rinkhals, coming back to the karretjie with meat he has scraped off the road or a porcupine he has clubbed.

Kapok will look at what he has brought and say, "No we can't use it, look at the maggots," or, "Yes, it's still clean. We can eat this."

When Kapok is happy, Fansie leans in and sniffs, making his nose crinkle and we all laugh. It is me who picks the meat off the skin to make a pot of food.

He knows what I can use and he bursts with pride when I say, "Dankie vir die kos, my seun."

We are here. Right on the edge of the town. "Run! Hide!" I want to shout, but Kapok will not listen; my children don't understand why I am afraid. They all think we are fine. The donkeys strain, the chain goes loose and I know when Miskiet finds us he will kill me.

5 MISKIET

I want to go to their camp and take him for me. The thing is he won't listen because he doesn't know me. A boy like that, one who hasn't been to school, who runs and sleeps and hunts, doesn't obey his elders. A boy like that does exactly what he wants and thinks only of his own comfort. He will have to be tamed, slowly and with patience, like a wild dog. Food, money and cigarettes. That's what works on boys like him.

There is no rush. There is starvation in their faces. Kapok has come to look for work with the Boere who knew him. It won't be difficult to lure her children. A packet of chips, a five bob. It won't take much. Fifteen years and she thinks I have forgotten. She is hoping I have forgotten.

After all this time, Klein Muisie, I have never stopped watching for you. I knew you would be back one day, that you would bring him back to Leeu Gamka, and now you bring me a prize of three children.

She will have to be punished and, when that time comes, she will understand this must happen. She took my son. Now he will live here and I am looking forward to it.

"Father and son," I will tell him. "I can teach you things only a father can teach a son."

The two girls can come too and keep the place clean. Washing and cooking, plenty to do. That older one is rough but can be beaten right. Maybe she can be cleaned up and I will allow her to sleep in my bed with me. The little one will learn quickly who is in charge.

Klein Muisie's children will have no papers. That is for sure. She had no ID and her children will have no birth certificates. The boy I will register with my name. The government will know he is mine. I will take charge of him and I will draw his All Pay. The girls can be left.

My son looks fit and his arms are taking the shape of a man who will be strong. She is returning him to me now at a time when he is ready to take over his duties and help his father.

Tonight, when I go to their camp, I will tell her to walk into the darkness with me. She will come because she has always obeyed and, when we are far enough, I will cut her throat like a sheep. She is lucky, my knife is sharp and it will be over quickly. Kapok is a coward. His silence will guarantee his life. He won't talk. I remember Kapok, his fear was always bigger than his heart.

When it is done, the children will come home with me. Before I go to their camp, I will prepare a place for them to sleep in my house and I will be merciful and sharpen my knife on the rock at the back door.

6   KAPOK

"Oudtshoorn" is all I hear.

"We must go to Oudtshoorn." All these years nothing, and now, when I want to go to Leeu Gamka, she wants to go to blerrie Oudtshoorn.

That's the problem with Muis. If a person wants to go one way then you can skiet dice that she will want to go the other way. It's very blerrie irritating. She wants birth certificates and an ID for her and for the children.

"We don't need them," I tell her. "What are we going to do with papers with the children's names on them? Hey? What?" Next time she can't find newspaper to roll a skuif she'll be ripping off a piece of birth certificate to make a pil.

Dom blerrie woman. I would give her a klap just to show her who is baas but she's acting so quiet and strange I am just going to leave it and do what I want. Ek weet nie. Ek is so moeg and my leg is very sore. I don't have the krag to fight with her about this. "If the government knows about them then he can't do anything." She says it so quietly I can hardly hear. "If the government doesn't know about us he can hurt us. It's then he can take the children."

She says it over and over. It's that fokken Miskiet again. She is so scared of that bastard that she will have us running backwards and forwards to blerrie Oudtshoorn.

Muis thinks that while she is nie amptelike nie, with no face, he can slide a knife across her throat and finish her off, finish off a life that never was in the first place. The same goes for the children. They don't exist because they don't have birth certificates.

I tell her the Liewe Jesus knows about us, he will take care of the children, but she looks at me like she doesn't believe me.

"Liewe Jesus doesn't carry a knife. How's he going to stop Miskiet from doing what he wants to do?" she says.

Ag jissie, ek is te moeg vir die storie.

I am not scared of that blerrie bastard. He won't hurt me. In his eyes I will be just a useless cripple. A useless cripple who stole the woman he wanted and the newborn he had claimed as his son. But I did a good thing for Muis. It's been a hard life on the vlaktes, but I have seen her laugh and most of the time she has peace in her eyes.

But, Liewe Jesus, right now I am so moeg of hearing about him coming to get us and that all we can do to stop him is to go to blerrie Oudtshoorn. Sometimes I just want to leave them all sitting at the side of the blerrie road and take my donkeys and go. Maybe then I can have some rest.

Ja, look, he must have been angry when we disappeared. Hehe hehe! But I felt sorry for the poor girl, sitting under the pepper tree day after day, feeding her baby and not talking. I saw how he watched her and I guessed what happened to Jan. He wasn't killed by some blerrie darkie truck driver. That's what Miskiet said, that Jan was dead and the darkie was raping Muis when he found them. The ou ran away and took his knife with him. Miskiet said he was too shocked to chase after him. He saw his brother was dead and his brother's girl being raped and he was too scared to do anything. Ja-nee, Jissus. Like Miskiet has ever been scared of anything in his life. But he put on a good show.

"The darkie will come back for me," he told the police.

Muis never said a word but I can guess what really happened. When the police asked her to tell them she wouldn't talk. And *that's* when the skinderbekkies in Rondomskrik on the hill in Leeu Gamka started talking. When the baby came all those many months later, we all knew it was Jan's child. Poor Jan, to die like that in a filthy tunnel when you have a pretty girl with a baby on the way. Ek weet nie. Life is not fair. Shoo, shoo, shoo!

I remember how it was for me after Mina died. It wasn't the same on the karretjie. There is no joy in lighting a fire for one person at night, making coffee and skinning a rabbit with only donkeys to talk to.

Muis, with her baby in her arms, needed a ride out of town. She was like me, alone, with no one to talk to. I think she was planning to go back to her mother. It would have been a hiding for her if she came to the farm carrying a snot-brat and no man. Her father wouldn't ask questions, he would just give her a hiding to welcome her and the baby.

I wanted children but Mina was always too thin or too sick and it never happened. With Muis I saw I could have a woman and a child straight away and I liked the idea. That baby boy never knew his real daddy. It was me who was the lucky one. It is me who he calls Pappie now.

One thing. My ou Mina didn't nag like Muis. Oh that woman can moan and complain. Mina was relaxed. We just went day to day, not worrying about tomorrow. When Mandela came I thought about going to Prince Albert to vote but then I said to Mina, "What's the point? You vote for the darkies it's going to be the same as if you vote for the whities. They are not worried about giving us karretjiemense houses and cars."

Anyway, I like my life. I don't smaak living in a house in town and riding a bicycle. Mina was good that way; she agreed with me so we didn't worry about going to vote for Mandela in the end. For many years Mina and I drove our karretjie from farm to farm looking for work and we never went hungry. There was always a pot of something to eat. When I worked with sheep I bought afval which she curried with Karoobossie. Jissie, I can only smack my lips when I think of Mina's cooking. And a sheep's head, ek sê!

I remember her telling me, "Joseph (that's my church name), you dig a hole and I will make you food that will make your stomach so happy," she said. I dug a hole and she built up the fire and, when the coals were red hot, she scooped them in the ground with the spade and then rested the sheep's head in them. I covered the hole and the next morning, when I dug up that head, it was pitch black. I put it on a flat rock to cool and then I chopped it open with my hammer. Inside, the soft brain was cooked like bone marrow and with a little salt we spread it, lekker hot, on roosterkoek. It was the nicest food a hungry man could imagine.

Ag ja, my ou Mina. She died from the TB. In Mina's time the grass grew thick on the sides of the track and the springs in our secret places always had a little bubble of water I could dig out to make a drinking place for the donkeys.

Then it was, let me think now, Vaaltuin and Oortjies. Now those were good pullers and they could plough too. Ou Baas Steyn was so impressed when I ploughed his lucerne lands for him with my donkeys. "You did all that with those blerrie donkeys?" he said. Heh heh!

"Die kant, Oo-oortjies. That's good. Ja!"

"Kom Vaaltuin, maak klaar. Nee, nee, vorentoe."

At the end of the day I rubbed their grey bodies with a rag and they groaned with pleasure. Heh heh! Ja, Vaaltuin and Oortjies were good donkeys.

Where has the grass gone? When we stop at Heuningvlei now the spring is dry. It was never dry when Mina was alive but the water is gone and I can't dig to it anymore.

It's these changes every year. A little less water in the springs my father and grandfather showed me when I was a child. "Boesman secrets," my passed-away father said. He showed me where the bees hid their honey and how to make honey beer with just a few scoops of bran. Those beehives have gone too.

It's because the Karoo is changing that we have to go back to Leeu Gamka. No matter what Muis says, we have to. Pantoffel and Rinnik are just ribs with no strength to pull the karretjie. All we eat now is what the boy finds and it is not enough. We are all slowly starving, Mamma, Pappie, children, dog and donkeys. All of us, always so hungry.

All day the boy is out in front running with his dog. When he comes back to the karretjie with a bokkie or a rabbit his black eyes look in mine in a way that makes my heart go soft. His face is open, even with the scar on his cheek from that time he fell off the roof of Ou Piet's pigsty.

"Pappie, can we eat it?" he asks me.

I tell him he mustn't ever bring a tortoise. A tortoise cries only one tear and that is when it dies. I don't want to be the one who makes that one tear even if we are hungry.

When he can, he catches something, but most often it's a road kill that he finds. "Hayi!" I said to him the other day. "It's just as well these blerrie Boere drive like maniacs otherwise we wouldn't eat." That was the day we scraped a duiker off the Prince Albert Road. That's one road that always gives us something to eat when our stomachs really talk.

For the first time I am thinking I am going to have to sell the donkeys and the karretjie and find fixed farm work. I can work with sheep. I can make fences. I will find a job where there is somewhere to live and then we can eat afval and sheep's head every day.

But now this woman wants to go to blerrie Oudtshoorn. Instead of being invisible, like she wanted all these years, now she wants birth certificates and an ID book.

After all this time I don't think Miskiet will still carry hate in his heart. I know I wouldn't. Mind you, she does have this way of making a man very angry and every now and then one has to give her a klap to stop her mouth. She is sure he will kill her and take our children. Going to Oudtshoorn will be protection from him. Ja, maybe she is right, but it won't protect us from our hunger.

7 FANSIE

Rinkhals finds it. But I get it out. An aardvark hiding deep in its hole. It is a baby and we are going to eat it. I grab it by the leg and pull. Rinkhals is barking and barking and I think the thing is going to hurt me with its nails. Unlucky for him his hiding hole is shallow and I get him out easy. I know what an aardvark means and I am scared I will lose it because my hands are wet and slippery from sweating. When I have it out the gat I flip it on its back and it goes mad hitting at Rinkhals with its claws. Rinkhals tries to bite it but the aardvark is too fast even with me hanging on its tail.

Lucky for us Pappie hears the shouting and barking and comes running. When he sees what we have he shouts: "Hold tight, hold tight." He stands on its head with his thick boot shouting all the time: "Don't let go, Fansie, don't let go my son."

I am so excited and my heart is beating fast. I am so happy he says I am his son, even though it's not true. Mamma told me my blood father died protecting her and then Pappie saved her life by taking her away. Both ways I am lucky.

I hang on to the aardvark, feeling the tail twisting and turning in my wet hands. Pappie kills it with his panga, chop-chop, one slice across its throat and I can let go.

When it is all over I can feel my heart gallop like a donkey being whipped. I hold my hand on my chest until I can breathe and Rinkhals stops barking.

What this means is that tonight we are going to eat lekker! Mamma says she is going to braai it on the coals.

"Fansie, there is a lot of good meat on an aardvark," Pappie says. Jissie, I am so hungry I want to braai a piece now but Pappie has taken the thing and made Witpop sit by the fire with a razor cleaning the hairs off its body. Pappie says he thinks he can make Sponsie nice shoes from the skin. Aardvark skin is strong, but this one is a baby, so it's still soft enough for her little feet.

Mamma is cooking the heart and liver for us to eat now. Lekker. When Witpop is done Pappie will soak the rest of the meat she cut up in a bucket with vinegar. After it has finished soaking, when we have settled down in Leeu Gamka, we'll rub the leftover meat with curry powder and Karoobossies to keep the brommers off and hang it on the fence to dry. I am so happy that aardvark showed itself to Rinkhals so we can eat.

When I am alone I talk to the animals in the veld and ask them to show themselves to me. I don't tell them I want to eat them but I think they know that anyway because they always run when they see me. Early in the morning, when the sun is looking up over the veld, is the time the animals show themselves. Not the snakes and likkewans. They like the sun in the late afternoon. Nobody in my family likes the snakes and likkewans but I don't mind them. They always get out of my way if I shout at them.

"Go snake, go. Voetsak!" If I meet a cobra by surprise he always stands up and looks cross. Then I stand still as a tree or a rock. His black tongue goes in and out and his black eyes watch to see if I move. If I can stay still then he just goes down and slides into a bush as fast as he can. Puff adders I don't like. They are so fat and lazy and they don't like waking up for anybody. If you stand on them then you are finished. I just go around them. Puff adders are windgat.

The snake that makes me most afraid is the rinkhals with its black shiny body and white collar. If that snake bites you, you will be dead. Straight away. When I got my dog Rinkhals he was black with a white stripe on his neck and I knew his name was going to be Rinkhals. He is clever and he always helps me catch food. Once he even took a lamb. Pappie was very cross when I brought it back, but he still ate it.

"It's dead now, what must I do?" he said. "But pasop. If the Boere catch him killing their sheep they are going to shoot first and ask questions later."

After Pappie said that I was a bit scared but, if I know the Boere aren't in the veld and I am alone, I let Rinkhals catch a lamb. Then we make a fire and we eat it alone, just the two of us.

Last week I saw kudus that had come down from the mountains. That was when I wished I had a big shotgun like the Boere because I aimed and fired five times with my kettie before they galloped away. There was a bull, with long horns, watching me from the top of the koppie, and five cows. The meat on that bull would have fed us for weeks and weeks. Pappie could have made biltong and we wouldn't have had to come to Leeu Gamka and Mamma wouldn't be so quiet.

We are here now. She kept us away from this place and, in the end, it turns out to be a nothing place with just a few houses, much smaller than Prince Albert. Of course there is a big church with a high steeple and a bell. It's Sunday today and when we come in from the veld we hear the bell ringing. Pappie says it's calling the Boere to come pray.

I don't know why Mamma hates this place so much. It is okay here with the Ultra City and the big trucks. I never saw so many big trucks before, so I tied a string around Rinkhals' neck to keep him safe. Pappie says they come from all over the world and they are taking loads of food to people in Cape Town. Maybe one day I will ride in one of those trucks and also go to get some of that food in Cape Town.

We came in on the dirt track through the lokasie to the uitspan. It was early when we arrived and people were sleeping but the dogs still barked and chased us. Mamma said she wanted to get through the lokasie and set up camp before the skinderbekkies were on the street. There was one man watching us. He looked in my eyes, like he knew me, and I didn't smaak the feeling he gave me. I didn't say anything to Mamma. She's not talking anyway, so what's the use.

8 WITPOP

Sponsie was born in Rietbron under the donkey karretjie. We didn't know she was going to come on the night she chose, so I was sleeping at Didi's place and watching 7de Laan. I love TV. My Aunty Diksop says when I watch my mouth hangs open and they could hit me over the

33

head with a spade and I wouldn't notice. On the night Sponsie came I didn't tell Mamma I wasn't coming home; I just curled up on the floor by the TV and fell asleep. It was too dark to go back to the uitspan anyway, so I stayed, even when Didi's brother, Kobus, kicked me and told me I was a stinking karretjiemeid.

When Pappie came the next morning to tell everyone Sponsie was born I was so sad I wasn't there because I really wanted to see how a baby is born. Tears just jumped out of my eyes and everybody laughed at me.

"Ja, you don't want to go back to your donkeys, stinking karretjiemeid, then that's what happens," Kobus said. Aunty and Oom were talking to Pappie so they couldn't hear him. I walked to the tap and drank water so I could get away from him. I didn't chirp him but I thought, ja, you come with us Kobus, come with this karretjiemeid into the veld and see how useless you really are.

The next day my bleeding started and Mamma said it was the shock from hearing my sister had come and me missing the birth. Now I want soft pads wrapped in pink plastic. This business of making balls out of *Die Son* and sticking them in your broek is not lekker. The whole day all a person can think about is what's in her broek because it's so uncomfortable. No really, I want a pink roll-on, a lappie and soft pads. I think you can buy this stuff in Leeu Gamka. There are shops, although there is no Pep like in Prince Albert. I like Pep; you can buy everything at Pep, even hair extensions. Once Mamma bought elastic bands and made my hair into little balletjies called popcorn. It was sore but at least I didn't have grass growing out my head for a few weeks. I know I am a stinking karretjiemeid. But even a stinking karretjiemeid can like shops, can't she? I like the smell of soap and roll-on. I also like pads. When we are in Prince Albert I smell the stuff in Pep. I don't care that the Boere complain about me. There's a nice aunty working in the Pep in Prince Albert. She lets me smell first and then she chases me outside.

Fansie caught an aardvark yesterday so we are all feeling strong today after eating last night. If he hadn't caught that thing I am not sure we would have made it into Leeu Gamka. But still the donkeys look as though they are about to vrek from hunger. Can we eat the donkeys? No really, I do think about eating them. There have been days when I have had dreams about braaing Pantoffel and Rinnik. S'true. Ja, but Pappie would die before he let us eat his donkeys.

Mamma says I must shuddup about pads and pink roll-on because we don't have money for flour and yeast so she can't worry about me nagging for stupid stuff. I know that. I know we are starving but a stinking karretjiemeid can dream. Dreams are free.

We came through Leeu Gamka this morning when people were sleeping. I saw one oom fast asleep in his yard holding his papsak in his arms. I think he was dreaming about a woman because he was doing the sex move with his hips. Ag wat! Like I said, dreams are free. Fansie and me laughed and laughed and then Fansie shouted "Dronkie! Dronkie! Dronkie!" to wake him up but Pappie told him "Shuddup!"

That's the one thing I don't like when we come to town. Papsak. First thing Mamma and Pappie want is a wyntjie. No matter how hungry we are Mamma sends Pappie around looking to get her a dop. I hope they don't give away the rest of Fansie's aardvark for a papsak. That's why I didn't go home that night Sponsie was born. They had a papsak and they were going to be happy or they would be fighting. Also there was nice stuff to watch on TV. When they fight Pappie klaps Mamma in the face and tells her, "Your bek moves too much. Shuddup." Once Mamma ran after Pappie with the spade and klapped his kapok leg. Eina! Many times. When Pappie can't move his leg then Mamma runs around for him, bringing him coffee and chopping wood while he sits and watches. She feels bad, s'true, I can see that.

We are in Leeu Gamka now with the fire burning and some of our aardvark on the coals. Pappie has gone to look for a doppie for them. When he comes back the party is going to start, that's for sure. Maybe tonight it will be a good thing. Maybe a doppie will make Mamma talk a bit and feel happy again.

9 MUIS

There was a stone pressing into my cheek when he held me on the ground. If I touch my cheek I can feel the spot, even after all this time. It didn't bleed but it must have hurt the bone on my face so that I can still feel the pain easily. That time of year in Leeu Gamka, when he held me down, the heat makes waves, like water, in the air. If you look over the veld you see water moving even when there is nothing there. It was late afternoon when it happened.

I walk from the red brick house on the hill to the highway. The new blue plakkies Jan bought for me when he got his pay are hurting my toes but I can't stop looking at them. They are the first shoes that are all mine, from new.

"They'll take the shape of your foot in a day or two then they won't hurt," Jan said.

The hot ground doesn't burn me now when I walk and I don't have to stop all the time to pick duwweltjies out my feet.

"One of these days I will buy you real sandals with straps," Jan said to me. "The plakkies are just for now, so you can come meet me when I finish work."

When I came from Fraserburg, three months before with my brother Danie, on our father's donkey karretjie, I came with nothing on my feet. All I had was my spare doek, my mother's white comb and a half a jar of Vaseline. Danie dropped me at the side of the highway in Leeu Gamka and pointed to the houses where I should look for a job. We had left Gansvlei, the farm where we were born, when Meneer Van der Westhuizen told my father his adult children couldn't stay anymore.

"There are too many of you here now," Meneer Van der Westhuizen said. "The big ones must go to town and find jobs."

The big ones. That was Danie and me. My mother cried and my father gave us his karretjie and told Danie to bring it back when he found work and had money for his own wheels. Nobody told Danie to look after me, even though I was a silly girl. So now I was alone in Leeu Gamka looking for a job.

Danie said he was heading to Beaufort West, but that was too far from my mother for me.

"Leave me in Leeu Gamka, I'll let Mamma know where I am and that I am not too far," I told him.

I thought Danie would stay to help me but he didn't. He just dropped me off on the highway and then sloered on with my father's karretjie. For a long time I watched his round back on the karretjie. He never looked back, he never waved good-bye. In the end, when I couldn't see him anymore, I walked into the lokasie and asked the first person I saw the way to the church. It was a plain, white little building with three steps in front. I sat on the steps until Sister Nina saw me. It was a Pinkster Protestant Church, and I knew they were kwaai. She was glad for a new soul, she said.

That first night Sister Nina gave me a place to sleep and food. "Leeu Gamka is no place for a dom plaasmeid," she said. "You had better stay here in my safe arms until we can find you a place of your own."

I was so grateful that I did all her washing and turned her house out every day for three weeks until Jan noticed me. He gave me my first job. For a R5 and a plate of food I had to clean the house he shared with his brother, Miskiet, and do their washing every day. Also I could sleep on the kitchen floor, which was off the street. Jan was a kind man with a good job as a petrol-jokkie at the Ultra City. Every day he bought me little treats. It was with Jan, under the pepper tree in their yard, that I drank Coke for the first time.

"You mean to tell me they don't have Coke in Fraserburg?"

"We were on a farm, far from town," I laughed.

"Was there no Coke in the farm shop?"

I thought about it for a while. There were bright red bottles of Groovy but no Coke.

Miskiet, Jan's brother, hung around in the yard, listening to us talk but he never spoke to me. I was afraid of his silence but I made his bed and washed his clothes. All the time he watched me. When he smiled, it was to himself, but I kept my head down and worked hard. The best part of the day was when Jan arrived home from his shift at the petrol station.

"Hullo Muisie, come see what I have for you," he would call and I would come running like a child for the treat he brought me. Sometimes it was half a packet of chips, or wine gums or a blikkie Fanta.

And then I started walking to the Ultra City to wait for Jan to finish work. We would walk hand-in-hand, laughing and sharing what he had bought with his tips.

On the day Miskiet held me down, Jan bought me a one-litre Fanta all for myself because I was so thirsty. He said I mustn't drink it in the front because Meneer De Wet was around and he got the moer in with the petrol-jokkie's girlfriends hanging around.

"You go on, Muis, wait for me by the tunnel and save me a sip."

That garage is busy with big trucks driven by blue-black drivers coming from far away and going to Cape Town with their loads. It is interesting to watch them and wonder where they are from.

I walk slowly with the bottle of cooldrink, lifting it now and then to press the coolness against my face.

At the tunnel I stop. Where does he want me to wait? There is a nice sitting place on the other side, on the hill, so I run down the steps, enjoying the smacking of my new plakkies on the cement.

In the half light, with the sound of trucks above, I see Miskiet leaning against the tunnel wall. I feel sweat run down the inside of my legs and my hands go wet but I carry on walking, looking at the ground.

As I pass him he leans forward and touches my shoulder. I don't know what to do. He spins me round and presses his lips on mine. The Fanta bottle drops out of my hand and breaks. I try to pull away and one of my plakkies comes off. He pushes me down on the ground and I close my eyes and feel the stone pushing deep into my cheek.

Jan came like he said he would. I heard his voice, felt the weight lift off me and I crawled to the wall and opened my eyes but all I saw was the silver blade. I only opened my eyes again when old Oom Dollars shook my shoulder. It was then that I saw my hopes and dreams bleeding into the dust in a tunnel that stank of pee.

10   MISKIET

My bloodied sheets are bleached and on the line. I don't like blood on my sheets. The early morning sun lights up flecks of dust as I sweep the floors. Everything feels in order now. I waited and they came. Things will change. On the floor next to my bed is Jan's old mattress. The boy will sleep with me; Muis's two klimmeide will sleep in the kitchen on cardboard. I have found some old boxes and flattened them and piled them in the corner. I am ready.

My blade winks and blinks on the table. It's a big flick knife with a blade as long as the length of my hand and a brown plastic handle. It's not rubbish that will break easily. It won't let me down. It hasn't before. The day I bought it, there were two in Mevrou Smit's drawer at the general dealer in Prince Albert. I knew when I saw them, between rolls of ribbon and hair elastics, that it was one like that I wanted: a man's knife.

"This'll cut biltong nicely," Mevrou Smit said when I gave her R35. "My husband has one and he finds it very handy for cutting biltong." The old woman showed me how the blade sprung out when you pressed a little button on the side.

"You hold that button down with your thumb to fold the blade in again," she said. I could see she liked that knife. She handled it like she had been playing with it when she was alone in the shop.

It slid into my jeans' pocket comfortably. That's what I liked about this knife. A person could walk all day with it resting on the top of his leg. It was in a place where I could touch it easily and that made me calm. Nobody knew what I had in my pocket, that I could take it out and flick the blade any time I wanted.

It was Klein Muisie, sleeping in her clothes on our kitchen floor, who made me buy the knife. If it wasn't for her, Jan would be alive and the blade wouldn't blink and wink at me all the time.

The first night, when Jan brought her home, she lay down on a flattened cardboard box in front of the stove. I felt her there straight away; the breathing in our house changed.

Then, a few nights later, I heard Jan swing his legs out of bed and creep into the kitchen and lie down on the floor with her. The breathing was fast, then slow. Every night, when he thought I was asleep in the bed next to him, I heard the springs in his mattress creak as he swung his legs over the side and stood up.

She stayed with us for a long time, washing and cooking, but in the dark my brother became a tweegatjakkals who lay on the floor with her, making me feel like an unwanted Jappie in my own home.

The knife was a way to discipline her, to make her understand that it was my house, that I knew what they were doing, and that it would stop when I decided.

One day when Jan leaves for the early shift at the Shell, I put my arms around her waist and pull her against me so she can feel what she is doing to me, but she pushes me away.

"Leave me alone, I am your brother's woman."

"You are our woman," I tell her. "There are two men who need looking after in this house."

"Sies, you disgusting pig," she says.

I take out the knife. The blade flicks open and I hold it at her throat. It is good to see the fear in her eyes. She will learn to respect me.

40

There is nothing that makes me angry more quickly than a dom plaasmeid with a fight in her eyes.

I know now what I will do.

She wouldn't lie with me in my own house, on a bed, in a decent way, so I decided she would give me what I wanted in that vuil tunnel near the Ultra City. It was easy to follow her. Easy to know what Jan would do. I never wanted it to be that way, but afterwards I knew it was the way it had to be. You cannot do something like that under your brother's nose and not expect him to feel angry. It was that plaasmeid who changed everything.

She is back now to pay for her crimes. That is why she has come back here.

After Jan was dead, I told the police it was one of those darkies who drive the big trucks. I told them he raped her and killed Jan. She knew better than to point a finger at me. Even after all these years, the police have never knocked on my door.

"Shame, poor Miskiet," the people said. "Who will take care of him now? Those brothers meant everything to each other."

I expected her to go straight away, but she stayed, like she expected Jan to come back. Then, when the baby was born, he was no darkie. He was yellow and soft just like me. Nobody asked Mevrou Smit in Prince Albert who bought her knives or if they were only used for cutting biltong.

11 WITPOP

Mamma loves Fansie more than me. S'true. It could be because he is a boy and brings us food or it could be because I am a girl and make her stressed because I don't have ears. She always says that. "Jy het nie ore nie. You don't listen."

Fansie runs like a kudu through the veld. He runs for hours and nobody worries about him and when he comes back everybody is happy to see him because he always has a porcupine or a rabbit for supper. If I disappear like that Mamma hits me with a stick when I come back. Really, she does.

"Where have you been? I can't do the washing and look after Sponsie" or "Why were you gone so long, where is the firewood, hey?"

Hit, hit, hit. If I cry it's like she wants to hit me more. Eina! Eina! Eina! Whack, whack, whack.

Once I tried to run with Fansie but he threw stones at me so I came back to the karretjie. When I run by myself Pappie shouts, "Witpop, come back here." So now I walk alone next to the karretjie all day watching the mountains and singing.

My hartjie, my liefie,
die son sak weg,
die son sak weg,
die son sak weg,
daar onder by die Blouberge.

Sometimes I change the words and sing "Daar onder by die Swartberge" when we are close to the Swartberg. It's stupid to sing about blue mountains when you are walking next to black mountains. Also the sun doesn't go down over the Swartberg but I sing that it does anyway.

To run and hunt animals and never wash clothes or look after a baby or collect stokkies must be a feeling like being God. To have a mamma who looks at you with softness in her eyes when you come home must make you feel like a giant. When Mamma looks at me, it's always with a plan on her face. Like, what can Witpop do now? I try to stay behind her so that she can't always be thinking of things for me to do.

She loves Fansie the most of all of us, maybe even more than Pappie, but that could be because Pappie's leg is too stiff for him to catch food anymore. She's proud of Fansie. When he comes home with a porcupine or, like yesterday, when he dug out that aardvark, her face shines with happiness. Actually, I am glad he finds the food otherwise we would be eating fresh air with leaves. They don't have any money for food and Pappie is always looking for work. Mamma won't work for money; she has to stay with the karretjie and keep us hidden and safe.

But she moans all the time.

"Kapok, you are walking our legs off. No meat, no bread, just walk, walk, walk."

She could get All Pay but we aren't registered with the government, so we don't get anything. You have to register your children if you want to get pay. Mamma wants the money very badly but she doesn't want to register us and she also doesn't have an identity. I don't know why, I just wish she would get All Pay so that I could have a lappie and a pink roll-on and pads.

Today I decided that one day, when I don't have to tramp behind their karretjie, I am going to live in a town with shops and eat chicken and rice every day and drink tea with sugar from a glass cup. Really, that's what I am going to do. I am going to have those brown, glass see-through cups that Didi's mamma has. Didi says she bought them at Smit's Winkel in Prince Albert. I am going to get All Pay and use my money to buy some of those brown glass cups from Smit's. And a lappie and a pink roll-on and pads from Pep. Really.

Mamma makes nice food with the Karoobossies and the meat Fansie brings, but if you ask me what my favourite is, I say chicken stew and rice. Chicken tastes like town. It's soft and easy to chew, not hard and bony like the rabbits Fansie brings. Once we asked people for their empties and made enough to buy big red slippery Russians from the shop at the garage. Really, that's my other favourite thing to eat. Those big red worsies.

If I think about it, Mamma loves Fansie the most because he brings food and his real pappie is dead. In her heart she feels sorry for him because he is half an orphan. Fansie never knew his pappie because he died before he was born. Mamma says he was a good man who loved her and he bought her plakkies. My pappie also loves Fansie very much. He is always saying things like "My son, help me here please" or "My son, you will learn to shear sheep one day".

I don't know why he calls him "my son" when he is not really his son. It is because he is a boy. That's what I think.

Mamma and Pappie never call me "my daughter". They just vloek me and shout "Witpop, I am going to bliksem you if you don't do what I say" or "Witpop, what is your problem?" That's all I ever hear. That I have a problem. And they don't know what it is.

Fansie thinks he is the boss of me and Sponsie. He has also started coming with this: "Fetch wood, fetch water, I am going to hit you."

Nobody sees, but sometimes I sit a little way from the karretjie on a flat stone between the bushes and I let the tears roll down my cheeks. They are hot and feel nice when they come. When I sit alone I have time to feel where they hit me, on my back, across my legs. Today, when I wouldn't carry Sponsie, Mamma hit me across the face.

12   MUIS

I would be happy if I could never come back to this place. What is here but sadness? What is here but fear? He says it is the only place where he can find work. All these years he found work in other places but now he thinks we will starve if we don't come back to this place. As the donkeys pull us closer I see the red brick houses on the hill. Big trucks pass on the highway to Cape Town. There is the Shell Ultra City. Nothing has changed. There are very few trees in Leeu Gamka.

From far away I can see the old pepper tree where Jan and I used to sit, where I sat with Fansie after he was born. It's the only tree I can see.

The chain around my ankle tying me to Leeu Gamka is loose. For so many years I have been like a dog pulling to break free. Now, after all this time, I have raw sores where this chain has cut through to my flesh. Kapok thinks I will lick Miskiet's hand, then lie at his feet asking for forgiveness. The one who raped me, the one who took away the only person who cared. I never wanted to see him again. I never wanted to remember. Here I am, at the beginning again. The donkeys are pulling me closer until we are at his house. The red brick house where I slept on cardboard on the floor.

Kapok is sure he can find work. Baas Kobus will fetch us in his bakkie and take us all to Genade.

"I know people in Leeu Gamka who will help us," he says.

"He will kill me."

"When we have money we can go to Oudtshoorn and get birth papers and your identity."

"He will kill me."

"No, he has forgotten you."

"He is waiting to kill me."

Kapok does not know the part of Miskiet that I fear. Kapok has not looked into his eyes when he has decided something and you know you have to do what he says. What Kapok knows is the smiling, smoking, talking Miskiet. I know the man who smells of spray, who takes my arm in a way that I cannot escape, who looks at me with black staring eyes that make me move without him saying anything.

I want my children to be registered and have an identity before he finds me again. I think about this all the time and I know government papers can be my protection. If you have an identity, the police know when you are killed. They ask questions like: "Here is an identity, but where is the person?" They say things like: "This person has gone but their identity is here, we must find this missing person." If you have no identity then they don't know you are gone and they don't look for you.

"When you die nobody will even know you existed." Words he hisses in my ear as he pushes my face into the dirt.

When I thought about what he said I said to myself, "But other people will miss me, a life can't vanish. Somebody will know I died from a slit throat and a killer is out there."

Then, as if he can see all my thoughts, he says, "In court the police have to prove to the judge you existed. If they can't find your body and you have no identity how will they know it isn't all a big lie? Klein Muisie, the time will come when no one will ever know you were here."

We are in Leeu Gamka now and, when Miskiet finds me, he will kill me.

13 KAPOK

If he comes we'll drink wine together and Muis will see her worry is for nothing. There is a R25 papsak under the karretjie seat that I bought at the shebeen on the edge of town. I have had a little smakie already. Heh heh! Just a little sippie. Ag jissie, it's been a long time since I felt my arms go lam and my legs just want to sit down. Tonight I am going to suip and my friend Miskiet is going to suip too. What I am waiting for is that deep sleep that only a papsak gives a person. A papsak sleep makes the ground feel like a soft bed and my wife's ugly face look like an angel's. Heh heh heh!

Oh, my leg is so blerrie sore.

Muis is scared of Miskiet but I told her she should not be afraid, she should feel sorry for him. That kind of person you just talk to and soon their anger turns into dust and, when they see you have a papsak, then you are pals for life. Wait. Tonight I will make Miskiet my pal for life.

Really, I don't know why he would be angry at me for taking Muis off his hands. She was Jan's woman with Jan's baby. I don't know why he wanted her so much. If a woman didn't want me I would let her go. A man must have a woman who likes to stay with him. Even if she moans and complains, like Muis does to me, in her heart she must want to stay. But Miskiet would not take no for an answer. In the end all he got right was to make himself cross and Muis unhappy. If you think about it, it was dom. Before Jan came from Beaufort West, Miskiet lived very quietly in that red brick house in Rondomskrik on the hill. The other people didn't smaak him. They said he was a malletjie with eyes that looked right through you. He was always alone, walking in the veld even in winter when the freezing wind cut at his face. Then back again in the afternoon. His hands were always in his jeans' pockets. Sometimes he would take one out and wave at me sitting under the pepper tree smoking my pipe, but he never stopped to talk. There were other times when he looked at me but I could see he saw nobody under the pepper tree. There were times when he would be gone for two or three days and when he came back he was dirty, with grass and sand in his hair from sleeping on the ground. That was the thing with Miskiet. You knew when he had slept on the ground. Most of the time he was clean and shiny. His hair was oiled and his yellow skin was scrubbed. When he went into one of his strange moods then he became dirty and deurmekaar. He is someone to feel sorry for, I tell you.

"That guy needs a nice girl to look after him," I told old Oom Dollars.

"He a malletjie," the oom said. "The nice girls is scared for him."

"I don't know why, he just goes a bit funny now and then. He won't hurt them."

"*I* am scared of him," Oom Dollars said.

I didn't feel scared of him but I didn't bother him either. A person doesn't want someone like Miskiet in his life if he can help it.

Then Jan, his brother, came from Beaufort West, and we all felt better that he at least had someone to talk to. Jislaaik, but Jan was a lekker outjie. He was always laughing and popular with the nice girls in Rondomskrik. When Muis turned up and needed a job he was quick to take her in. We could all see he had his eyes on her from day one. I wondered how it was going to work in that house with the three of them. Miskiet was so peaceful when he was alone and now all of a sudden he had his brother and a woman sharing a room with only a curtain between. He never complained, well, not to the men smoking pipes under the pepper tree.

The day of the killing, it was old Oom Dollars who found Jan in the tunnel. And Muis, rolled into a ball with her eyes shut tight.

"Who did this? Who did this?" he asked, shaking her, but she looked at him like she couldn't see, even when he was right there, in front of her. She wouldn't stop crying. The smell of blood and sex was in the tunnel, Oom Dollars said, all mixed up with Fanta Orange.

When the police came to question her she said niks. But Miskiet knew what had happened. He said it was a darkie from the trucks who raped Muis and killed Jan. I could see that. The dom meid, she was always hanging around that Ultra City, smiling at Jan and drinking cooldrinks with the petrol-jokkies. One of those trucker darkies must have smaaked her. But they never found who it was.

Jislaaik, it wasn't a nice time.

I wondered how Miskiet would cope after the killing. Shame man! Poor bliksem didn't ask for all this drama in his life and now he had a dead brother and a woman with a broken heart.

We all thought she would go back to her people in Fraserburg straight away, but she didn't. Then, in a few months, we knew why. She was expecting. A girl who is expecting can't go home to the farm, her father will beat her black and blue. She stayed and I wondered if Miskiet would make her his woman. But people talked. They said Muis

48

slept in the hok at the back waiting for her belly to grow, thinking what she could do. She wouldn't let Miskiet near her. That's when I knew it was him. He killed his brother and raped Muis in one of his rages.

So that's when I thought she would be a nice one for me. A plaasmeid with a baby would suit me fine. I like babies. I wanted to look for work on the vlaktes. My hands needed to get busy again. Too much blerrie sitting around gets you down. She was sitting under the pepper tree feeding the baby when I asked her if she would come as my woman. What I wanted was a person to talk to and someone to cook.

"Ja, dankie, dankie, Oom Kapok, ja I want to come with you on the karretjie." She was so happy when I asked her, like it was the chance she had been waiting for all this time.

I was pleased.

"Just promise me one thing?" she said.

"What?"

"Promise me we will never come back here."

Ag jissie, I wasn't really going to promise that. Leeu Gamka was my home. But I said, "Ja, it's a terrible place this. I will take you to the mountains where there is water in the river and lots of trees to sit under."

"Just get me away from Miskiet to a place where he can't find me." I looked at her to see if she was being funny, but her face was so sad that my heart did a little jump.

"Okay, I'll make plans," I said. "I'll come tell you stilletjies when I am ready to go."

But now, all these years later, I can't understand why she is still so afraid of Miskiet. She moans so much about us having no work and no money – I thought she would be glad to come back here to regular pay and a once-a-week braaisak instead of a plat porcupine for supper.

And now, since we arrived, she hasn't said a word. Miskiet is almost family to her, but say his name and she goes doodstil and when you look carefully you see her hands are shaking.

And this blerrie Oudtshoorn thing. All this time, at every place, all she wanted was to vanish between the koppies. She didn't even want to come near the farms where I worked. She would make me uitspan two or three kays away until she saw exactly who was there and then kruip closer with the children. Now, all of a sudden, she wants to go to blerrie Oudtshoorn for birth certificates and ID books and I don't understand why it is important.

But here we are in Leeu Gamka. The one place Muis said she never wanted to see again. Maybe, as she gets older, she is becoming less hardegat. She's here but her whole body is shaking. I told her "Relax, man. Leave him to me. Tonight we are going to suip and by tomorrow Miskiet will be my best pal."

14 WITPOP

Tonight we are sleeping in the veld. Fansie told me to get the blanket ready and make sure Sponsie ate something so she wouldn't cry. If she cries and they find us then it is hit, klap, kick till Fansie tells them where he's buried Pappie's fence-making tools. When Pappie buys a papsak then Fansie always buries the tools. If he doesn't then Pappie and Mamma sell everything when the dop hits. Last time Fansie forgot the pliers and Pappie traded them for half a papsak.

One time, when I was very little, before Sponsie was born, Mamma was very drunk and tried to give me to a man for another dop. Really, she did. Fansie screamed, "Run away, Witpop, run!" That time Mamma tore my shirt when she tried to grab me but she was too drunk to catch me and the papsak-man was too drunk to chase me so I didn't have to run far. I sat in the dark for a long time listening to them fighting and then singing.

"Witpop? Witpop?"

I jump when I hear Fansie's voice.

"Witpop? Where are you?" He finds me in the dark.

"You mustn't let her give you to a man," he says. "If that happens again and I am not here then you must run away and hide until the dop is out of her."

In the moonlight I can see his eyes shine.

"A man will take you away from us and hurt you and then, when the drinking is finished, Mamma will be sorry about what she has done."

I nod and lean in closer to him. He is sitting on the ground next to me and his arm goes around my shoulders and I feel safe. For the rest of the night we sit in the dark laughing at Mamma and Pappie fighting and dancing like real dronkies. At last it is quiet and we sleep together between the stones and the bushes.

In the morning, before they are awake, we dig up Pappie's tools and lay them carefully in their place under the seat of the karretjie. We run together to find Pantoffel and Rinnik in the veld. Last night Fansie chased them away too. Otherwise, he said, they would also be sold for a papsak and the two of us would be pulling the karretjie.

"It's the wine talking," he says. "They don't know what they are saying and when the wine is all peed out they can't remember anything."

I am glad he told me that.

Tonight we are sleeping in the veld again because Pappie has a papsak.

"It's to settle this business," Pappie says.

I don't know what the business is, but we all know there is going to be a lot of drinking and fighting. Mamma's eyes are different today, like deep pools of black mud. She looks, but she doesn't see. If you talk to her she doesn't hear you. When the sun starts dropping in the sky I make Sponsie coffee and bread and then, when we see Pappie pouring wine into his cup, we walk off quietly, disappearing like jackals into the night.

15 MISKIET

Klein Muisie, after all this time, I am paying you a visit.

Ducking and diving between rocks and bushes for fifteen years hasn't helped you hide. In the end you had to come back to see what life you missed, hey? If you knew how I dreamt of feeling my fingers around your bony throat. I want to push a lap in your mouth and see the fear in your eyes as you wait for death. It's a funny thing but my mind can be busy with something like dominoes or cards when, out of nowhere, it settles on killing you.

It's because you ran. You took my son and ran away when I was ready to be his father. You were disrespectful. You were disrespectful and now you are going to pay.

Tonight I will visit you in your camp. If I know Kapok he will be gesuip, singing to his papsak. Useless piece of shit. With Kapok it's always about a dop and I am sure you are the same. Oh yes, I am sure you will be drinking too. Kapok and Klein Muisie come to town and the first thing they want is wine to make a party. You can't help it. Too many long weeks away without a doppie, hey Klein Muisie? There comes a time when that doppie becomes more important than anything else. I know that. I have seen it many times. By sunset Kapok will have sold his draadtrekker for R25. You won't even notice what he has done because the two of you will be wiping out the pain of your rubbish lives with cheap wine. But I'm warning you. I'm telling you now, that pain is only going to get worse now you have turned up on my doorstep again.

Look at you. Filthy. All of you in rags carrying on like rats running in the veld for food. So useless you can't stay in one place long enough to find out the clinic hours or put your name on a housing list. You can't even get All Pay because you can't get to a town on the right day of the week to register your children. So they stay nameless and always hungry.

My son can live and eat with *me* now. I waited for him to come back and I knew one day he would. You should never have taken him away. If he had stayed by me I would have fed him and bought him toy cars and ice-lollies.

And you, Muis, you could have lived with me and my son in my house on the hill.

I would have been the one in charge and you could have kept the place clean. Omo-smelling sheets would have flapped on my line; lamb stew would have cooked on the stove while my boy played with wire cars in the dirt at the back door. And, when he saw me trekking up the hill after work, he would have run to meet me and hugged my legs and shouted "Pappa's home". He would have run behind me and cried that I went to the Ultra City without him.

Now, he is going to come and stay by me. That is what I have decided.

My son will be with me. He will sleep in his own bed and eat at the table with his father. I will teach him to slaughter a sheep and tighten a fence. In the evenings we will play cards and drink tea with three spoons of sugar and milk.

It's dark now but I know every turn in this path. I pick my way quietly and easily towards you. You and Kapok are alone in the uitspan on the far side of the highway. For a while I sit on the koppie and watch you.

Klein Muisie, you know I am coming. I can see you sitting on an upturned tin staring into the fire.

Kapok doesn't sit. He moves around adding wood to the flames, then walks to the edge of the ring of light and stares into the dark. Then he scratches in the donkey karretjie and finds a tin which he sets down next to the fire. An empty seat. An invitation to your party. The children are gone but I know where they are. Hiding in the veld and watching the camp, just like me. The donkeys are missing too. I stand up and stretch.

Okay, Klein Muisie. The time has come.

16 FANSIE

Tonight I saw the man again, that oompie who watched us from his red brick house when we came this morning. Even from where I was hidden I could smell his spray. When Pappie washes he smells like wood smoke and Lux and we tease him by running up close and sniffing him and screaming. Even Sponsie was doing it last time. It was so funny seeing her run on wobbly legs, laughing and sniffing Pappie. His body always looks so small and krom when he takes off his shirt and shaves with a bowl of soapy water balanced on the seat of the karretjie. Pappie buys his blades at Pep Stores when we are in Prince Albert. Blades and carbolic soap. He likes to shave and he hates a blunt blade.

This man in the red brick house is much bigger than Pappie. I checked him. That oompie has eaten lots of boerewors because he looks lekker strong. When I spied him tonight his jeans looked new and very blue and he had black All Stars just like the ones Kobus, my cousin, wears. I don't need All Stars. I go barefoot because my feet are strong.

After standing for a few minutes the oompie came out of his house, locked the door with a big gold padlock and pointed his nose to our camp. At the gate he turned and went back and checked the padlock again, pulling it twice to make sure it was really locked. I thought about climbing into his house. He locked it with a padlock but I could just lift the plaat on the roof and jump in if I wanted.

When he came out I didn't move. When you are stalking an animal you must move very slowly. If you move the animal sees you from the corner of its eye and is gone. If you stay still it can smell you but it can't see you. Sometimes it will come right to your feet. Then you have to move fast, like a cobra, to catch it. It's the same with stalking a person. This oompie is easy to track – I saw straight away where he was heading and that Mamma and Pappie are waiting for someone. It looks like it's him.

He walked with a spring, like someone on their way to something they are really looking forward to. Even in the dark I had to run to keep up. He headed straight, along the edge of the lokasie, along the koppie path to the tunnel under the road. When he got to the tunnel he looked back. I think he wanted to be sure he went in alone. It's got a strong feeling, that tunnel. When I went in there, I didn't smaak the feeling, so I climbed up to the bank and crossed the highway. Just before the oompie disappeared, jumping down the tunnel steps two-by-two, he looked back up at the koppie, his eyes moving over me as if I was a rock. When he was gone I walked along the highway and watched the big trucks for a little while. On the other side I could see Mamma and Pappie by the fire; the oompie wasn't with them. Then I saw him, on the other side of the highway, sitting on a rock watching our camp.

It was a strange night. For once Mamma didn't shout and tell us we were all useless and lazy and that she had to do all the work. She sat like a little mouse on her tin with a far-away look in her eyes like she was thinking about something deep inside her. If you got her attention then she looked at you like you were a spook and her hands started shaking. I didn't smaak having Mamma like this. I told Witpop there was trouble coming and that she must take Sponsie and go and sleep in the veld. She better listen or I am going to cut a big stick from a pepper tree and piets her backside. That Witpop will leave Sponsie sleeping under a bush and creep back to camp to listen to what is going on.

At last the oompie stood up from the rock where he was sitting and walked down the bank to our uitspan. He walked into the camp and went straight to the fire and kicked the coffee-pot into the flames. Just like that. It was fresh coffee that Witpop made so they wouldn't start too early on the papsak. Even though he did that Pappie said nothing, just handed him a mug of wine. I ran over the highway and scrambled down the bank into the circle of light. The oompie saw me and smiled. There was something in his pocket that he touched all the time. When he is drunk, I'll take it.

17 MUIS

A jackal is circling our camp waiting to snatch his prey. When a person lives in the veld for a long time you feel the air change when another creature is close. So many times I know a snake is there before I see it. The cobra under the bush where I want to pee never surprises me, and the hissing of the puff adder lying next to the rock where Sponsie is walking warns me to grab her into my arms. It's the same now – the air has changed. There is movement around us, I can hear the hiss.

Sponsie is crying in the dark and Witpop is saying, "Shhh, shhh." Fansie is nowhere.

"Take her away, Witpop. You are too close. Move off, hide, hide away in the night. Use your brain for once," I whisper.

I shift my weight on the old paint tin where I am sitting by the fire. My legs are stiff from holding the same position for so long. All the time I have been sitting in a way that I can jump. Then, from the corner of my eye, I see a movement, a flash of Fansie's T-shirt disappears towards the crying and shhhing. Has he been here all the time? When Sponsie cries again it is a far-away weeping. She wants her mamma's titty on the blanket in our place under the karretjie.

My stomach, my head, my shoulders ache with waiting. Waiting for hitting and kicking. I stretch my legs in front of me and take a deep breath. Kapok hands me a skuif and I drag hard. The tobacco smoke burns my lungs and my head feels light. When he comes will he punch my face and then go for my guts? If I fall will he kick me and then take a rock and bash my head? Will he rape me?

Kapok is wrong. This jackal, this snake, this murderer, hasn't forgotten about me. He is coming back to show me he is stronger, that he is powerful and that, in the end, he will be the winner. All those years ago he wanted to be in charge of my life but no person will do that to me. Mamma taught me that I belong to Liewe Jesus and, in my life, I decide what is right and wrong. In the end I must stand before the

Liewe Jesus and answer for what I have done. Nothing says I have to answer to Miskiet.

I have stayed away from here so I can live but, in the end, it is my children's hunger that has brought me back. Sponsie crying for a piece of bread, Witpop snatching at kaiings, Fansie's black eyes looking for a chance to eat. This is what made me come back to Leeu Gamka. These children and their hunger are eating out my heart. We can die of hunger wandering up and down langkampe in the Karoo or I can have my head bashed in by a killer who is not right in the head.

This is the only place where Kapok knows enough people to find work quickly, this hard, struggling place of suffering called Leeu Gamka.

There are footsteps coming. They stop but I don't move and I don't look up. He has been on the bank near the road watching us. Kapok built the fire big so that there is enough light to see him coming but I don't want to see him. I can smell his spray and soap. It's his same smell, like bleach mixed with spray from Pep, the one I remember, and it makes my stomach turn over and I want to be sick.

When he comes it is with big fast steps and he kicks over the coffeepot on the fire. Fresh coffee that Witpop made.

I know he is standing next to me. He laughs softly and says, "Hullo, Klein Muisie."

My eyes move from the fire to his black tekkies. I can see a pattern on his green socks.

Kapok says, "Hullo Miskiet, are you going to join us for a little wine?"

He takes the wine cup Kapok is holding out and sits on the paint blik that Kapok has prepared on the other side of the fire, facing me.

"Is Muis not having anything?" he asks. Kapok hands me a cup of wine and I take a long sluk. Why not face death drunk? I sluk again and hold up my cup for some more.

When I look up, I see Fansie is on the other side of the camp behind him. Miskiet glances over his shoulder and, when he sees the boy, he stands up and walks towards him.

Fansie, go, go, go.

"Leave him alone, Miskiet." For the first time my voice doesn't fail me. "He is Jan's boy."

I shout the words and they hang for a long time over the silent veld. Fansie has vanished like a duikertjie in the dark, and Miskiet laughs and comes back to the fire for more wine.

18   FANSIE

Pappie sold the saw to Oom Dollars for R25 so he could buy a papsak. Next time he gets a job he is going to ask the farmer for a voorskot, a little money in advance, so he can buy a new one. That's what he said to Oom Dollars.

"Tonight I need the papsak more than the saw," he said. "Tonight this papsak is an emergency."

An emergency is when you can't wait for something but have to have it now, now, now. For me food is an emergency, but I don't have a saw to give for bread, so my emergency is happening all the time.

When Pappie has a papsak he is in a very good mood, and even before he takes a slukkie, he swings his hips and claps his hands above his head. Witpop and Sponsie and me all laugh and dance with him.

"Suikerbossie, ek wil jou hê. Al sou jou Mamma wat ook sê!"

If Pappie has been working then sometimes we have money for radio batteries and we dance to RSG. When he starts dopping I watch him. For a while he stays funny and wants to dance but then he gets cross and then it's better to go sleep in the veld. Even if he calls, "Fansie, bring stokkies for the fire," I stay in the veld or he klaps me for sports, saying I took too long or the stokkies are too green or there are not enough. When he has been dopping for a while, everything, this whole damn life, is my fault.

When the wine is finished he and Mamma sleep. In the morning, before they wake up, Witpop, Sponsie and me go back to camp and make the fire and, if there is any, we make coffee. When they open their eyes they don't remember anything. They just have a moer of a babalaas and want coffee straight away. Mamma says another doppie would help her head but there is never any left over.

On those nights, when we are alone in the veld, we make houses. It was my game to make Witpop shuddup so she didn't want to run back to Mamma when they were drinking. If she went back when Mamma had a papsak then Mamma klapped her or, like one time, she tried to give her away to a man for a papsak. That's why I hid Witpop, and now Sponsie, just like Pappie's tools and the donkeys. I hide them away and keep them quiet until they stop dopping.

It's easy when there is a big moon, then we can see better, otherwise we just let our eyes grow used to the dark and we build houses. We each make our own house with little klippies for the walls. When Sponsie wants to sleep we put her in one of the bedrooms. She likes to choose which house she is going to sleep in and we have to make her a bed and give her pretend food and then she always falls asleep very quickly. In my house I have a bedroom, a kitchen and a TV. Witpop makes me laugh because she makes a room for a car in her house.

"You have never even been in a car, now you make it a whole room. Are you a larney?"

"My car is a fancy red one and I don't want it to get damaged so it needs its own room," she says. She spends a lot of time washing her car too. Like she saw our cousin Kobus do one time for the Boer on the farm where he lives.

"Why don't you make a room for the donkeys?" I ask her, just for a joke.

"Donkeys don't sleep inside, they will kak everywhere."

When she says this we laugh our heads off, thinking of Pantoffel and Rinnik in their own room.

When we are tired I invite her over to watch *7de Laan* on my TV. Witpop loves *7de Laan* and we talk about the programme and the news. Then she gets us coffee before we say good-night and go to our bedrooms to sleep. The problem is our houses don't keep the goggas out. Once when I was sleeping in my bedroom, a scorpion stung me on the arm. It was a big sore for a long time but Pappie rubbed aloe and ash on the sting and then, when it had been sore for a long time, it got better and went away.

Tonight Witpop wants to build houses but I can't relax and so I shout at her, "Why do you always want to do baby things when big people's things are more important?"

She cries when I say that and she and Sponsie make a little camp by brushing all the stones and rocks away from where they want to lie down. Then they go to sleep. When I look at her she's sucking her thumb, with Sponsie lying in her arms. Witpop can be so stupid sometimes. Everything is just games for her.

This oompie visiting here tonight is lekker cross, but when he came into camp I saw Pappie was very clever and gave him wine quickly to make him happy. Maybe later he will dance and find a place to sleep by the fire. But this oompie is not like the others. He's got something on his mind and even though he is taking a dop I can see he is not in the party mood. Pappie has rolled him a skuif now and is trying to talk to him, to get a chat going, but the oompie is ignoring him, drinking wine and smoking.

I was scared when he got up and walked over to me so I ran away to Witpop. I don't smaak this oompie but I am behind him now, keeping just out of his sight. Mamma can see me. I follow the wet shine of her eyes in the dark but she has been careful not to show that she can see me.

He is on his feet. There is a click and a flash and I see he has a knife. So that's the thing he was touching in his pocket.

What is happening now? What is he going to do? The blade is out. He is going to steek Mamma.

19 MUIS

A klap always gets me when I don't expect it. One minute I am sitting enjoying a dop and the next I am on my back like a tortoise with a boot going at my head or my back or my guts. Sometimes I think there is something about my face that really makes men the moer in. When I was small my pappa said I had a cheeky face with attitude in my eyes. That attitude got me a lot of hidings. I just had to look at Pappa and he would be standing up, loosening his belt.

"Hester," he says to my mother and he's dragging me across the room by my ear, "this blerrie klimmeid doesn't want to hear."

Once when I was very small Mamma tried to stop him but the belt came down on her back when he was finished with me. After that she didn't ever stop him again. She told me I must stay out of his way and not look at his face. When he was very angry Mamma would feed me at the back door and tell me to sleep in the bush until his bees were back in the hive. My pappa had a lot of bees living in his head and, jinne, when they came out you didn't want to be around.

But Jan was a good man. In all the months I lived with him he never hit me, even when I had an attitude. He didn't have any bees living in his head. He only drank Fanta and that's most probably why he didn't get the moer in so quickly. Jan would have been a good pappa for Fansie. Someone who smiled and brought him sweets and not a pappie who hit and chased him.

When I think about it, I can't be too angry with my pappa. Life is very hard, especially when you are working sheep, and a person feels like a little doppie at the end of the week. It's a pity that a doppie makes some people want to kill someone else. It was a big pity that that someone else was me, with my cheeky face.

I also like a wyntjie but I don't want to kill anyone. I want to be happy and dance to forget my troubles and then sleep. The best feeling is to be in the mood for a party and to dance and sing and then sleep.

Kapok takes a dop too when he has money. Then his bees come out and I get a few klaps because it makes him feel like a strong man. But he is not so angry as my pappa used to be. Really, if you want to know the truth, I think Kapok is scared of me. Once I threw boiling water in his face when he hit me. His face looked bad for a long time, with the skin peeling away and half of him was like a whitey. I would never have done that to my pappa. No way, jinne!

Tonight I am getting a big hiding. I know that. This hiding is the one Miskiet has been waiting a very long time to give me. This hiding is going to be one of those death hidings, where the man giving it wants the woman getting it to be dead when he is finished. Aunty Loos had one of those hidings from Oom Japie. Oom Japie was my pappa's brother who lived with Aunty Loos on the farm with us in Fraserburg. Afterwards, when Oom Japie was finished with that hiding, we buried her in the veld on the farm and the police locked Oom Japie up for a long time before he was back, giving a new aunty the same hidings as the ones he gave Aunty Loos.

When Miskiet comes tonight I feel like one of the mice Fansie catches and keeps in a box. No matter how much I want to run away I can't find a way out. Fansie lets his mice go but I don't think that is going to happen to me. Now I am watching and waiting for his bees to start buzzing and then for the kick from his nice clean tekkies. My bones feel small and my skin is black from walking in the Karoo sun. Why does he bother with someone like me? I am not important. I am nothing. I can't read, I don't have money, I just walk this way and that way across the Great Karoo with my children, a sick man, two skraal donkeys and a dog. If a farmer chases us, we go. If a car comes, we pull out of the way. If we see people, we turn another way. But this Miskiet won't leave me alone and he has become the devil watching my life.

Go away, Miskiet. Find a woman who dresses in shop clothes and cooks white people's food. I don't want to die. I don't want you to kick and klap me until I am bleeding out my mouth and nose.

But now, a blade shines in the firelight and I close my eyes. It is coming.

When he hits me I fall back on the ground. Ja, I think as I am falling. Ja, Kapok, I told you he wouldn't just be happy to suip with you. I feel the weight of him on top of me and I smell dop on his breath. Is this how a sheep feels when it has its throat cut? I feel my shoulders scraping on the stones. He is so heavy. I can't breathe.

"Muis? Muis? Kom."

The weight is off me but I keep my eyes closed tight, waiting for a kick.

"Muis. Kom."

I open my eyes and look at the stars. Kapok and Fansie lift me on to my feet and I hear Kapok telling Fansie to bring in the donkeys and fetch his sisters.

"We are going to blerrie Oudtshoorn tonight," he says.

Miskiet is lying next to me with blood coming out his mouth. His eyes are closed. Kapok is using his knobkerrie as a walking stick. His leg always gives him trouble when he sits too long.

"We can get away if we leave now," he says.

Miskiet's hand is closed around his knife. I look at it and think that knife is the same one that killed Jan.

20   KAPOK

A man can't inspan donkeys when he's had a dop. Jislaaik! My fingers
don't want to work and I can't get the buckles up so I just push it all
into Fansie's hands and I hold the donkeys still. Fansie is a real little
bliksem. He sees I am struggling with the buckles and that we are in a
rush but he just watches me. Even though I have a maybe dead man
lying next to my camp fire, who I have bliksem'd, and we are about to
make a run for it, he doesn't say anything or try to help.

Now, when I tell him, his young boy hands do the job quickly.

"Kom, kom!"

He uses a knee to push Pantoffel into position in front of the karretjie.

"Staan!"

"Skuif!"

Both donkeys back into the karretjie. He is good with donkeys and
they listen to him.

Miskiet hasn't moved since I hit him. Even though it was dark I saw
blood dripping into the dust near his mouth. He is lying on his side
with one leg folded over the other and one arm stretched above his
head. I bliksem'd him so hard he is surely dead. And you know what?
I don't care. He can blerrie vrek. He comes into my camp acting like a
grootmeneer, kicking my coffee over and not saying a word and then
trying to stick a knife in my woman. If he got that right, what am I going to do with her children?

"We should pull him away from the road into the bushes," I say to
Fansie. The boy stops what he is doing and looks at the body, then
shakes his head.

"He just looks like a dronkie who has passed out. Leave him."

Tonight, when I saw the knife, I knew he had come to murder. Muis
was right, he hadn't forgotten. The first chance and he wants to slag
her. She is still standing on the spot where Fansie and I pulled her to
her feet, moaning. No words, just moaning like a baby.

I bliksem'd Miskiet without thinking. He was going to kill Muis and I stopped him. And now a big man with a knife is lying next to the road and he's maybe dead because I hit him. The knobkerrie was next to me when we sat by the fire, then in my hands, above my head, then it came down so fast I didn't have time to blerrie think. My ears roared when I cracked it down. Still now my heart is beating fast and I can feel thundering in my ears. "He's not dead but he might die because I hit him as hard as I could," I say to Fansie.

"You must have cracked his kop," says Fansie. The karretjie is hitched and the klimmeid has loaded all our things. For a few moments she and Fansie stand, and in the moonlight I can see them looking at Miskiet. "If he dies the police will come for us. We must run now," I say. "I did it because he was going to kill Mamma."

"Let's go away, Pappie," says the boy.

Witpop's girl voice says, "If he was a porcupine we would be braaing now."

"Sies, Witpop. It's not right to talk about a dead person like that," the boy says. "Shoo, how can you say something like that?"

Then she starts laughing and Fansie too. Blerrie children. Their pappie has cracked someone's head, their mamma is not lekker and they are laughing.

It is too dark for me to see Miskiet's face, but I bend over his body and feel for a pulse. I can feel it beating.

"He is not dead."

"No, and when he wakes up he is going to have a moer of a headache and he is going to be looking for us. Kom, Pappie, let's go now," says Fansie.

Muis's moaning becomes louder and Fansie helps me lift her into the back, where Sponsie is already fast asleep and wrapped in her blanket. Muis lies next to the girl, curled small, and now she looks like she will sleep too.

Fansie gives me a hand up and I take the reins. The two children move up front, whispering to the donkeys, and we move off, onto the gravel road, and then we are heading for the far-away mountains. I look back once and see the body, still there in the dirt. Very soon the lights of Leeu Gamka are like lost stars behind us. The roar of the trucks fades and all we can hear is a jackal yelping far away in the veld. After a while I slow down to let Witpop up into the karretjie.

"Where are we going, Pappie?" she asks.

Before I answer I look over at her mamma, still curled like a baby, but now crying quietly in the karretjie.

"Blerrie Oudtshoorn," I say, loud enough so Muis can hear. "We are going to get you birth certificates and your mamma an identity."

21 WITPOP

For Mamma to get an identity she needs a picture of her face and she doesn't know how to get a picture. Aunty Diksop told me that we have to go to Prince Albert on the day the government comes to give identities and they will sort out a picture. The problem is that the government comes so little and we never get it right to be in town on the same day. Really. You tell Pappie he must be in Prince Albert on a Monday and he looks at you skeef.

"What day is it now?"

"It's Monday, Pappie."

"But then we must be there now."

"No, Pappie, next Monday."

"No man, I can't worry about next Monday on today's Monday."

Really, it's very hard to get Pappie to understand.

It's because of all this that we don't get pay and we don't have birth certificates and Mamma never gets her identity. If we did get pay, then Mamma said I could have money to buy a pink roll-on, a lappie and pads from Pep. I was so happy when she said that, it was like I had these things in my hands already. All I could think about was that one time when I went to Pep and the lady there let me smell all the roll-ons. The Pep lady said the pink one smelt like roses. Didi told me that roses are flowers, like a vygie.

"They are big white and pink balls and they only grow in Prince Albert because they need water. They are too soft and sweet for this hard veld."

Didi told me that next time we are in Prince Albert I must look at the museum if I want to see roses.

"They have pink ones there that smell just like roll-on," Didi said.

Once, when Didi was in Prince Albert, she asked Kobus to steal a rose from the museum for her. Really, he did it. He pulled a pink ball off one of the bushes and brought it to her. She said afterwards he was the moer in because he didn't know those pretty balls had thorns and they pricked him very sore. Didi keeps the rose in her school Bible. She showed it to me and even though it was brown and hard it still smelt a bit of roll-on. She wouldn't let me touch it.

"Your hands are too hard for it," she said.

If we went to Prince Albert I would try and be brave enough to smell those white and pink balls at the museum, but I am sure someone would chase me now, after Kobus pulled one off. Then, I thought, maybe Fansie could take me in the night and I could steal a rose too, even though I don't have a Bible where I could keep it.

After a few days of thinking about roll-on and roses I changed my mind. What I really want with my pay is school shoes. Shiny new ones. I can see them in my head. They must be black with a buckle on the outside and cut-out flowers on the toes.

"Mamma, when we get our All Pay, I think I must get school shoes first."

"That's a good idea," she said. "At least your feet will be warm in winter."

It was decided then. I would get school shoes.

"Can I have a pink roll-on, a lappie and pads the next month?"

"Yes, yes, you can have those things the next time."

Pappie said he would teach me to polish my shoes with his special shoe brush.

"My father taught me to keep my shoes shiny," he said. "If you keep your shoes shiny they last longer and they are softer."

When I get my new shoes he says he will cut out board from an old box and put it inside to make them last longer.

I was so happy when he told me that I couldn't stop smiling and Fansie got cross.

"You are not going to get stupid shoes because we don't get pay because Mamma doesn't have an identity," he said.

"Leave her," Mamma said to him. "Leave her to think about her shoes and her spray."

"Not spray, Mamma, roll-on."

Mamma didn't hear. She was already walking off to look for stokkies.

I could feel tears coming in my eyes and I also walked into the veld, pretending to help look for stokkies but was really so that they couldn't see my sadness.

I want to be a town girl with shoes and roll-on and a Bible with a rose. And I want to go to school and learn about one-two-three and letters.

We can be deep in the veld, far from any town, and Pappie still brushes his shoes every day. Pappie wears brown shoes, with long laces, that Baas Johan bought him from the koöperasie shop when he worked on Tierberg. He has polished those shoes so many times that the heels are red and the leather soft. Now that I am planning my school shoes I sit with him every night when he cleans his shoes to see how it's done.

"To get your shoes really shiny you must spit on them," he tells me.

"Really, spit on your own shoes?"

"Watch me."

He spits on the shoe in his hand and rubs the spit into the shoe, whip-whap with the brush. That brush moves so fast over the shoe I can't see it.

"Whew, Pappie, but you polish fast."

"Practice, meisiekind. It makes perfect."

I don't know exactly what he means, but his shoes look perfect and mine will too if I polish them.

It started one night, when Fansie asked Pappie: "Pappie, when Mamma gets an identity and we get pay, can I also get black school shoes?"

Really, I looked at him as if he was mad but I kept my mouth shut.

"Yes, Fansie. Your feet are nearly as big as a man's feet now. Maybe we must get you koöperasie shoes."

Really! Fansie liked it when Pappie said that and his smile was so big I could see all his teeth.

I wanted to say, "Mamma doesn't have an identity and we can't get pay so how are you going to get koöperasie shoes, huh?" but his smile was beautiful and he was so excited that I didn't want to make him sad like he made me, so I laughed with him.

"You two are going to look like real larney klonkies stomping around the Karoo in fancy new shoes," Pappie laughed.

We both stood up and pretended we had our shoes on, walking around with our noses in the air. I gave my foot for Pappie to see and he pretended to brush it.

"Don't spit on my foot, Pappie," I said.

Fansie started laughing when I said that and then Pappie started laughing and me too. We were laughing so much we couldn't stop. Even Sponsie was laughing and I saw Mamma smiling and shaking her head.

Many times after that night I saw Fansie sitting alone staring into the veld and I knew he was thinking about his koöperasie shoes. His hands would move in a way that I could see him stroking the leather, then he would knock the air with a finger when he was feeling the thickness of the sole.

Every night we polished our shoes in our minds with Pappie. We sat with him and spat and rubbed even though we had nothing in our hands. Pappie said nothing. We just talked and laughed like we were all doing a job together.

But now, since we've been in Leeu Gamka, it's been different. Mamma is so quiet and Pappie just wants to find work, so he hasn't worried about shoes again. Then tonight the oom came and everything has changed. If that oom is dead the police are going to be after us in the morning. If he is not dead then he is going to come after us. One thing I know is that he will want his knife back. Fansie thinks he's clever, but I see him running in front with the donkeys and playing with that knife he took out of that oom's hand.

Anyway, we are going to have to run very fast to get away.

22 FANSIE

Tonight, after Pappie smacked the oom over the head with the knobkerrie, he said we are going to Oudtshoorn. I don't believe him. Mamma has been asking him for so long to go to Oudtshoorn so she can get an identity.

Every time he says, "Yes, yes, we'll go."

But we never go. Now tonight he says we are going to Oudtshoorn. Even if we go all that way I don't know how Mamma will ever get a picture. For an identity you must have a picture. That's the most important thing, so that the government can look at you and then look at your picture and say, "Yes, this is this person."

But Mamma doesn't have a picture and she doesn't know how to get one. Mamma also doesn't know when she was born, and a person needs to know that if you are going to ask the government for an identity. Her mamma told her she first saw the night stars at Buffelsgat on the vlaktes but she doesn't know where that is and we have never been able to find it. She also doesn't know the day or year. That's very important for white people who make identities. You must know the date and the year. You can't say you are fifty years old when you are only thirty years. The identity people want to know nineteen-something. And a month. January or July. Something like that and a number like 21 or 17 for the day. You must have a number. All Mamma knows is that she was born at Buffelsgat after her brother Charlie but before Vlooi. At least Mamma thinks she came after Charlie. That's what her mother told her, but she has ten brothers and sometimes her mother calls one Charlie and the other one Dusi and the other one Fillies. The next day the names are all deurmekaar and Charlie is Dusi and Dusi is Fillies and Fillies is Vlooi. It gets very confusing with ten brothers.

"I came easily into the world, never giving my mother any trouble," she always tells us. "Not like Vlooi – he nearly killed my poor mother coming out backwards and upside down." We laugh when she tells that story. Can a baby come into the world backwards and upside down? Jissie.

From the beginning of her life, Mamma has been a quiet, hidden-away person. That's why she is called Muis. She is a little mouse who doesn't make a noise and hides from snakes and cats and people. That's what other people think about Mamma Muis but, don't make a mistake, this Mamma Muis can bite. She gets very cross with me sometimes and then she chases me and tries to hit me, but I just laugh and run away. That makes her spit like a snake then I tease her and say she should be called Slangetjie not Muisie. I always see Pappie laughing quietly when we have these fights. Witpop makes her fed up too and then she is a very noisy mouse, shouting and swearing at all of us. Mostly, though, she is quiet and hides away when people come near us. Ja, but you know, what our Mamma Muis wants most in the world is an identity. A book that says her real name and gives the day when she was born and says she is a person who lives in South Africa. I think this will make her feel like she is a real person, not a mouse who must hide away.

Mamma's father was a donkey-cart man like Pappie, which is why she never went to school and why she doesn't have an identity.

"We would stay on a farm and I would go to school but then he would get fed up and we would pack the donkey karretjie and move again. In the end the teacher said I mustn't come back anymore," she says. She can't read and write letters. None of us can.

Mamma never went to school but she remembers everything about me. It was cold when I was born and she cried tears like rivers for my dead father and his new son. Ja, she told me, my father was dead before I was born and Pappie took me to be his own because I was beautiful. That's what Pappie says too.

"Fansie was brown all over with his eyes closed tight and hair that stood straight up." Witpop laughs and then Sponsie laughs because Witpop laughs when Pappie tells that story. They think it's funny that I had hair like a porcupine. It makes me very happy that Pappie chose me to be his boy.

Witpop was born after me but I can't remember a time when she wasn't here.

"Ja," Mamma says, "the flies drove me crazy when Witpop was born because it was so hot and she has been driving me crazy ever since." Witpop doesn't care when Mamma says that. She just looks at Mamma and gets a cross face.

Sponsie came in the cold too, like me. I remember that night not long ago. After Witpop and before Sponsie there was Meitjie but she died at that time when she was learning to walk. Like Sponsie is now. Pappie said it was her chest that closed in the winter and we had no medicine. I helped him dig a hole for her body. I remember, before we laid her in the hole, I took her little fingers in my hands but they were like cold stones. Then Pappie lifted her and put her body into the hole at the bottom of a koppie on the farm Skilpadberg and then we packed lots of rocks on top of the grave so the jackals couldn't dig her up. Afterwards Pappie said a prayer to the Liewe Jesus asking him to take care of our little sister. When he was done we all climbed on the karretjie and walked on, leaving her there alone in the veld in that gat. For a long time I looked back, feeling the tears coming fast over my cheeks. Mamma didn't talk. She just had that look on her face when her eyes go big and wild like an animal. She has never talked about Meitjie again. Our baby became a star that I sing to when I am alone.

"Meitjie is my baby, Meitjie is my darling girl."

I don't think I can even hum that song when Mamma is around. It would be too sad for her.

Pappie has the reins tonight and Witpop and me and Rinkhals are running in front with the donkeys. It's dark and these donkeys are very cross that they can't sleep so we are running with them to keep them moving. We have to keep running. That's one thing we two know for sure. Pappie is still gesuip but he's getting better with the cool night air on his face and the worry of the oom behind him. He thinks he killed that oom, that his heart will stop, and that it will be the police chasing us in the morning. But I know that oom isn't dead, and, if we are being chased tomorrow, it will be by him not the police. This time I think he is going to be very dangerous. His bees are buzzing in a big swarm looking for someone to sting.

Why does that oom want to bother us? We were not doing anything to anybody, so why did he come to worry us? Tonight he wanted to kill Mamma and it was like she had no fight in her when he pulled his knife. She was like a sheep after it's been caught and is about to have its throat slit. It just gives up struggling and lets the knife cut open its throat. Mamma is still lying in the karretjie, sleeping with Sponsie. She is not even trying to help Pappie keep the donkeys moving. "Run, Pantoffel. Kom Rinnik! On, on, on. Run."

When Pappie lets Witpop on the karretjie, I run alone in front and I take the oom's knife out of my pocket to have a look at it. It's a very sharp knife but the blade is inside. If I press a button it flicks out and then I push it in again. They never saw me take it but I think it is better if I have it and not the oom. He will want to get it back. That I know for sure.

23   MUIS

His smell is on my skin. It crawls over me like a tick looking for a place to suck. It's a smell that makes my mouth dry and my stomach naar. I rub my lips and nose over Sponsie's hair and her smell makes me feel peaceful. Her little body is curled next to me and she sleeps easy, even on the hard boards of the karretjie. The donkeys have stopped running now and their clip-clop matches the thump-thump of my heart. A yellow moon hangs over the far-away mountains. It's a long time until sunrise and the stars are bright. The big star is the one Fansie calls Meitjie's star. My little Meitjie, watching her Mamma shiver in the back of a cart as we run across the vlaktes, away from fear.

"It's not death I am running from, Meitjie," I say to her. "It is just I don't want to die being kicked and punched and stabbed, that's all. Are you waiting for me, Meitjie? Are you watching us?"

When I was little I gave the stars names. Girl, Spider, Porcupine. They all twinkled, no matter how my heart was breaking. My body is stiff and cold and I sit up trying to balance against the rocking of the karretjie. Kapok sees me and pulls the reins.

"Whoa, whoa." The donkeys stop and Rinnik snorts and tries to grab at dry grass.

I climb out and stumble into the veld to pee. There is no one else out here. This is an alone world. All that will be left of us tomorrow are our tracks. I watch the sky and think about the stars and the people who live in the black heaven, away from suffering.

Kapok has rolled a skuif and I go back to the karretjie and climb up on to the bankie next to him. We smoke without talking and then he picks up the reins. Sponsie is still asleep in the back. Fansie and Witpop take the donkeys' bridles and pull them on again. Kapok brings down the whip and we move off, slowly.

Everywhere I am aching. The skin inside one arm is broken and stings from where he dug in his nails when he grabbed me. My head throbs and my backside aches where I hit the ground when he shoved me. We carry on during the night, listening to the creaking karretjie until Kapok breaks the night silence.

"The donkeys must rest. We are near Tierberg now."

Kapok knows these tracks and we go through a farm gate with a board swinging on a pole and begin the long trek to the farmer's house. The road is sandy and many times we all push the karretjie while Fansie talks to Pantoffel and Rinnik, telling them, "Pull, pull."

"Baas Johan will give me something for the donkeys to eat in the morning," says Kapok.

Kapok likes Baas Johan. He strung wire for him here, before Sponsie was born.

"Baas Johan has got a soft spot for a donkey," he says.

"Remember when Pantoffel and Rinnik ran away?" I say and he chuckles.

"Blerrie donkeys. They ran all the way to the Beaufort West road."

All night Kapok followed their spoor before he saw them on the other side of the highway.

"Ai, these donkeys!" Kapok laughs when he remembers that day. "Baas Johan came looking for me, but I was already on my way back and he said, 'I can give you a lift, Kapokkie, but the bakkie is too small for two blerrie donkeys.' When I got back to the farm he let me off to sleep. Ai, blerrie donkeys."

At last the farmhouse appears in the grey morning light. Kapok stops the karretjie next to a windmill with a dam and a drinking bak.

"We'll uitspan for the rest of the day," he says. Fansie and Witpop unhitch the donkeys and the animals walk off to roll in the dust before drinking.

"Not too much water," Kapok shouts to Fansie as he walks towards the house. "Watch for their stomachs."

A little more and Fansie pulls up their heads and chases them off. When the donkeys are settled, eating dried leaves and seeds off bossies, the children make a fire on the far side of the dam. They don't want us to be seen from the house. Maybe Baas Johan will be angry we are here and we'll have to go.

We have some coffee, but no sugar, and a little bread flour and yeast. Witpop looks at me and I nod. "Make bread, we can eat."

Kapok squats at the back door of the house until Baas Johan comes outside. I see him pushing his hat on, ready for the day. There are others too and I can see Kapok talking. He knows people here.

For a long time I sit by the fire and let Sponsie drink. Fansie and Witpop are quiet, moving around the uitspan looking for stokkies to make krummel coals. Witpop brings me bitter coffee. Fansie is hungry but he says nothing. I can see from the way he moves he is ready to move off to find something for us to braai. Then he is gone and Witpop is working the last of the bread flour into dough.

She leaves the white ball in our bowl, with a wet lappie covering it, to rise in the morning sun.

Fansie will bring us something to eat. As I wait for Kapok to come, the chain tightens around my ankle and I feel Miskiet moving into our circle again. His voice is in my head and I can't make it shuddup.

"Your children don't exist."

"They have no papers."

"I can kill them."

"They won't be missed."

"Nobody cares you were ever born."

You can't kill a person and think they won't be missed. Other people know about us. But it's like he is right here in front of me, and he won't listen when I tell him he's wrong.

"The police don't look for someone who is not on the government's computer."

I must stop this thinking now. We are going to Oudtshoorn so we can get on to the government's computer. No more of this nothingness. My children have faces.

Kapok comes back with the scraping of a pap pot.

"We can stay today if I help with the sheep dockings," he says. "It's a good job, Muis. Lots of meat. The mevrou sent some pap for the children."

Fansie has gone into the veld alone. He wants to play with that knife he took off Miskiet. The one that was meant for my guts, which was in Miskiet's closed fist. Miskiet will get his hands on another one, I know that.

Witpop and Sponsie eat the pap while I sit by the dying fire, warming my hands around my cup and waiting to see if it will be the police or Miskiet who comes for us first.

24 FANSIE

The ground looks soft but I know it's hard and stony.

"Sleep," my head is telling me but my legs say "run".

All night we have run but now I need to be away from her fear. My legs have forgotten how to walk so they run everywhere. Why does that oom want to hurt her? Last night wasn't a nice run. Jissie, it was a hard run. Now I run easily through the veld between bushes, jumping rocks. At a sheep's water bak I sit down on the ground and stretch my legs in front of me. Thin brown sticks with old black scratches and scabs. The boereseuns have thick, strong legs with no sores. That would be nice, to have thick legs like a white boy who eats meat every day. If I had long pants then I wouldn't be covered in scratches and sores.

There is nothing I can do about my brown sticks. I don't take food when there is only a little, otherwise Sponsie and Witpop are hungry. Sponsie cries when she is hungry, a lot of small little sounds, not like real crying, and Witpop gets very cross. I would rather be hungry than have one sister going "waa, waa" and the other one shouting "los my uit, los my uit". Those girls give a boy a bad headache. Now I am hungry and my sisters are not here. Now I am a boy who wants meat and that feeling is making my eyes, ears and nose sharp. There is a rustling and a hare runs from a bush, one way then the next, before I can think of catching it.

"It's your lucky day, hare," I say softly. If Rinkhals was with me he would have caught it but I don't want Rinkhals here. I chained him to the karretjie at the uitspan to force him to sleep, otherwise I don't get any peace.

There is no water in this veld. Just a bak by the windmill for the sheep. If I want to catch anything it will be here where animals and birds come to drink. I roll over on my stomach and lie still. With my kettie I shoot two Namaqua duifies. First one and then, as its mate stands next to its body, I hit it with a stone too. I burn off the feathers and gut them with the knife I took from the oom. I cook the meat over a small fire from stokkies off dried-out bushes. The birds are so small I crunch right through the bones and spit out some burnt feathers. Afterwards I find a place to sleep, away from the water, out of sight. If the farmer checks this bak today he'll find me if I am too close. It's better to move off a little so I can sleep in peace. For a long time I watch the clouds making shapes in the sky. There is a tortoise cloud that looks like it is drinking from a watergat. One is a kudu spoor and another one is an old man with a beard and hat who looks like he is smoking a pipe.

Pappie is in my mind. He won't worry. If they move on I'll track them easily. He knows that. That oom is behind us. That's one thing I know for sure. Pappie didn't kill him with that knobkerrie. He's not strong enough to bring down a knobkerrie on a man and split his head open. Pappie thinks he is strong but I can see how his sore leg has made him weak. He didn't kill that oom. If he is not badly hurt, he will be after us. That oom is not lekker, but he is not the sort to go to the police. He doesn't want police to know about this thing he has with Mamma. That way if he kills her they'll know who did it. Whatever it is, whatever the reason is that he is chasing us, he doesn't want anyone to know. When I wake up I must check our back trail. That oom is following us, oh jissie, I can feel it.

In the afternoon a cold wind wakes me and I think about food again. There is soutbos growing near the bak and, like a sheep, I chew leaves. Then a duikertjie comes, picking its way through the bushes to the water. If I hit it between the eyes I can kill it. A stone is ready in my hand and slowly I aim, pulling the elastic back as far as it will go.

"TstTst."

It turns at the strange noise, its ears twitching, its little black nose sniffing the air. The stone flies. Today hunger makes me faster than this bokkie and the animal falls to its knees. I leap on it, bashing its head with a rock to make sure it can't run.

I have meat, I have food. My happiness is too much and I fall on my backside and sit with my dead bokkie between my legs. "Dankie, Liewe Jesus, dankie." Its warm sides twitch and I want to cook again. But then, when I see the oom's knife lying where I slept, I know I must go. Mamma needs this meat, so they can all eat. This duikertjie will give us her legs and make us able to run.

With the bokkie around my neck I move away from the mountains to the koppies far away. There is a fence between me and the ridge. A fence always means a road. It's the road we used to come into the farm. Our tracks from last night are still clear in the soft red sand. There are donkey droppings and my kaalvoet spoor. And then a long thin line that wanders like a dronkie from side to side. A dikwiel bicycle has come after us. A little way on, I find a Black Label bottle so new there are tiny drops of beer dripping into the dust. A person is nearby. I cross the road, climb through the fence and head for the koppies. They will give me a good place to see ahead.

On top, I sit with the duikertjie next to me and let my eyes move over the vlaktes and the mountains. Everything is still. Then, far away, I see a man and his bicycle on the track heading to the house. One of the workers, maybe. He stops and pushes for a while. Why is he off today when the farm is so busy? He must be a visitor. At the bottom of a small koppie he pushes the bike off the road, leaves it behind a bush and climbs. That man is checking the trail ahead. For a long time he sits and watches. I move down the back of a koppie, out of his sight. It's going to take longer but I'll go around the back of the house and come into our uitspan from the other side.

From so far off I will look like any klonkie to this man. As I run I know one thing for sure. That man sitting on the koppie is the oom. It didn't take him very long to find us, even with a sore head. Now I know he must be very cross and when he finds us he is going to want his knife. That oom is stalking us because he wants to make a kill.

When I arrive at the camp, it is nearly dark. I stand there trying to pull breath into my lungs. My legs are shaking from running so fast.

"The oom has found us."

Mamma and Pappie's eyes go wide. Pappie stops cleaning his pipe and Mamma stands up.

"Where is he?" asks Pappie.

"Sitting on a koppie watching us."

For a while nobody says anything. Then Pappie says, "We must eat as if there is nothing wrong. There are skaapsterte. They were docking the tails today. Everyone was given as many as he wanted. Eat, Fansie, tonight we do not go hungry."

Mamma has cooked them, still in their wool, in a large pot of boiling water. She fishes one out for me and I slip the meat and bone out of its woollen coat with one squeeze. Sponsie and Witpop have already eaten. They are sleeping, full of meat and so tired from last night's running.

"Mamma?" I say. She is quiet again but she smiles.

"Dis 'n mooi bokkie," Pappie says. "We'll clean it and carry on like nothing is worrying us."

After I have eaten my skaapsterte we work together with the oom's big knife. First stripping off the skin, then hanging up the carcass by the feet under the windmill. Rinkhals is so full he lies on his side, snoring. "We need to cut it in pieces and dry it on a fence," Pappie says. But we know tonight we will be running, not making biltong.

When we have finished washing the blood from our hands and arms Pappie says, "There is no moon. When it's dark we'll move off. There is a road around the back of the house. We must let the fire go down now and make it look like we are going to sleep." He stretches as if it is the end of a hard day and speaks quietly. "He won't come tonight, there are too many people here for murder."

25   MISKIET

I open my eyes. A bird hops on and off the circle of stones where they had their fire. The place reeks of donkey shit and stale wood smoke. It's a smell that glues itself to karretjiemense. I do not know how they stand it. Stinking human-animals, never washing, never changing their clothes.

For a while I close my eyes again. There is a bloody taste in my mouth and my ears are ringing. I must have bitten my tongue again. My head throbs. She was pinned under me. I had her. My knife was ready. And then blackness. That old bastard hit me over the head with something. When I open my eyes the bird is close to my face and I lift my hand to touch it but it flutters off and settles on the rocky circle again.

Be afraid, little bird. If I catch you my hand will close around your small body and squeeze until your tiny head hangs and beads of blood form in your nostrils.

What makes me sick is she has raised my son to be a filthy rat. He is starved, dressed in lappe, and the look of a jackal is in his eyes. When he is mine I will donder these karretjie manners out of him.

I can see him dressed in clean pants and an ironed shirt with new tekkies, the envy of all the filthy little rats scavenging in the lokasie streets. But she took him into the veld and now he is worse than they are.

Eina, my head is so sore. A big knop has swollen up and I let my hand rest on it. My hand falls back to the ground and I lie still. Trucks on the highway make the ground shake, making the throbbing in my head worse. One, two, then a car, three, four, five.

I push up on to my backside and sit for a while before I try to stand. He hit me hard, but not hard enough to kill me. He wanted to kill me. He should have killed me. Now he will have to die too. I would have left him before this. When I spit, it's all blood. For a while I stare at the red stain in the dust, but when flies land on it I get up.

My knife is gone. My flick knife that I bought from Smits that was so sharp and ready is in their hands.

The boy has taken it, ja. I can feel it. He wouldn't have left a knife like that.

Okay, have it boy. It is a present from your daddy. I have another one, boy. I have Jan's knife. Take my knife but you better know I am coming.

Tracking two donkeys pulling a karretjie isn't difficult. They won't move quickly. They can't.

When I catch up to them I will drag her into the veld and slap her bony face, this way and that way, this way and that way. She can scream, she can beg for her life, but this time she will fall to the ground and I will kick her useless. What I am looking forward to is taking a rock and bashing her face, and when the world finds her she will be a bloody, dirty, faceless nothing. She will lie for months in the Leeu Gamka mortuary and no one will know her name, and no one will know what her face used to be, and then she will be tossed like a dead dog into the ground so that the rest of us don't have to live with the stink. Or, even better, no one will find her in this wasteland and the crows can pick her bones clean.

My first few steps are a stagger. I need a drink of water and a wash. There is time for all of that, and still I will catch up with the slow donkeys and filthy karretjie-nothings who think they can run from me.

In the grey morning I walk back to the house on the hill above Leeu Gamka, through the tunnel and up the path. Ting-a-Ling's dog eyes me but it knows better than to bark unless it wants a kick. And today if it barks I will kick it to death.

In my house I wash my body carefully with a cloth and soap, and drink three pain pills. For a little while I sit on the chair in my kitchen. The window and the door are closed and I enjoy the quiet. I make sweet coffee. Then I pack a bag. Money at the bottom, tinned food, a can opener, matches, soap and spray. In my drawer I look at all my knives. The big one my daddy used to slag sheep is hard to carry. There are three little fold-away knives and then another smooth black flick knife that Jan bought from Smits after he saw mine.

I flick it open and study the sharp point. It has never been used.

Ja, Brother, when I flick your knife it will be so that I can stick it into the guts of your stinking whore.

26 MUIS

That first week, after Jan found me and took me to their house, I liked Miskiet more than him.

His things were on a little wood table by his bed. A small bowl with yellow soap, a plastic comb, a metal razor and spray that smelt so lekker. When he was out, I touched each item and put it back exactly the way he had them. My favourite was the spray. I liked spraying some and then sniffing the air. I had never smelt a thing like that before. My father and brother smelt of wood smoke and tobacco, sheep and sweat. But this roll-on made you want to keep on smelling.

When Miskiet and Jan came home from work they sat together by the fire outside, rolling cigarettes from newspaper and drinking coffee. At bedtime they both took off their clothes. Jan had a petrol-jokkie uniform and Miskiet wore a blue overall like an ordinary worker. Jan left his smart clothes on the floor by his shoes but Miskiet folded his and put them on a little shelf at the bottom of the table by his bed. Then they both crawled under their grey blanket, each on their own bed, and went to sleep. My pappa had the same blue overall as Miskiet and a grey blanket, but he didn't have a bed. In the summer, when it was too hot to breathe, Pappa laid his blanket on the ground outside the door and slept so he could feel the evening breeze.

In my new life in Leeu Gamka, away from the farm, I was cleaning for two men who slept high off the ground and washed with soap and used spray. It felt fancy, like I was working for larnies. Jan cleaned himself in the morning. His shift at the petrol station started before sunrise and he would wake me so that I could boil water for him to bathe. When it was ready I would say "Jan, your water is waiting" through the curtain that separated the kitchen, where I slept, and the room he shared with his brother. He would come through in shiny sleeping shorts, bare-chested and rubbing his eyes.

"Muisie, wait outside," he would say each time.

I would go outside and sit on an old Coke crate at the door listening to the splashing as he washed his face, then his armpits, his privates and last his feet. He'd dry himself with a small pink towel then dress in his petrol-jokkie shirt, blue shorts, tekkies, and a cap. Before he left I made him coffee and we sat together talking for a few minutes. When he was gone, I prepared for Miskiet. The plastic bakkie of Jan's dirty water I tossed on a small patch of grass. Miskiet wanted boiling water in two jugs next to the bak. His towel was blue and had to hang over the chair. Next to the plastic bak I laid out his soap bowl, razor, comb and spray, which he allowed me to take from his bedside the night before.

When it was all ready, I said his name softly. "Miskiet, Miskiet, you must wake up now. Your washing water is ready."

Then I went back to sit on the Coke crate while he prepared for the day. Sometimes I peeped through the back window and I could see him standing naked with his back to me, leaning over the bak and washing his face. He wasn't so skraal as Jan. When I peeped at Jan I just saw bones and stick legs. Legs like Fansie has now.

When he was dressed, he left the house without a word and I went inside to make their beds and sweep.

Miskiet looked smart and smelt nice when he went out. Jan told me his brother was looking for work in Leeu Gamka and that, some days, he hitched to Beaufort West.

"He wants a sitting-down job," he said, "and a car."

"He dresses smart enough for a sitting-down job," I said. "He should go to Cape Town on the train and get a job there."

"No, he won't go to Cape Town, that's too far away."

I preferred Miskiet because it felt like he was important. Jan talked to me and was friendly but he stank of petrol and his hands were always greasy, with black under his nails.

I thought Miskiet didn't like me. He listened to my small voice in the morning to wake up but otherwise he didn't speak to me. When he came home at night he ate the food I made but never said if it was good or bad. Jan always said my food was lekker, that I was the best cook, and he thanked me for doing a good job cleaning and washing his clothes, but more and more when Miskiet was there I felt like dirt on his shoe, like a piece of rubbish.

One day, a long time after I came to their house, just as he was leaving, Jan took my hand and brought it to his lips. I was so shy. I looked at the ground but my heart was beating and that night I couldn't wait for him to come home. When he did he brought me a can of Coke. We sat under the pepper tree and drank it together. After that I waited for Jan to come up the hill, singing or whistling as he came back from the Ultra City. Many times I walked to the petrol station and waited for him to finish and then we walked home together. All this time Miskiet said nothing. I knew I was just a meid in his thoughts. Someone to clean and make his food, someone he didn't see.

Then one night Jan came into the kitchen and I let him do what he wanted because it made him feel happy.

After that night I saw Miskiet didn't talk to Jan anymore. Before he said a few words, but now he said nothing and the silence was like a heavy rock on the house. He was always under the pepper tree smoking and watching us. It was this watching that started to drive me crazy in that house. Even when Jan came to me in the dark hours I knew Miskiet was awake and listening to our noises.

Now Fansie says he saw him watching again, from the koppie. When he said that, fear came at me like the water in the Gamka when it has been raining. My legs started shaking.

"He has found us," I say to Kapok.

"Ja, but he can't keep up on foot."

"Pappie, he has a bicycle," the boy says.

"Ag well, unless he has solid tubes he is going to have a pap wheel very soon."

Kapok laughs but I am thinking what will happen when he visits our camp the next time.

27 MISKIET

They are running now. Kapok's sjambok comes down on the donkeys, whipping them on into the night. Faster, faster, running for their lives. *It's no use, Kapokkie, I am coming. I am coming to catch you.*

Even in the dying light I can see the cart and its huddle of people shapes. They have a long way to go before they disappear and, even then, I will see the choices they make, no matter how fast those donkeys gallop. At the farm's southern gate they must go left or right. Right will take them to the Leeu Gamka road. They are not going to take that one. They will want to hide from me and that road is open, connecting farms where there is nowhere to hide. Left will take them to the mountains and the tar road to Oudtshoorn. That's the way they will go. They'll take that one and branch off at Klaarstroom and maybe go back to Prince Albert. The only problem with that road is there are no escapes. When they are in the Gang it will be straight or nowhere and I will be right behind them. They could go into one of the farms – Paradys has nice hiding places, but I would pick up their tracks easily. What they might do is take the Willowmore Road, this side of Meiringspoort, and head east. Kapok knows the Willowmore farms; it's shearing country and they need to eat. They won't leave the Great Karoo. With its side roads and farm gates there are plenty of places to hide on the Willowmore Road. Yes, that's what I want them to do. The Willowmore Road is a way into open space and loneliness, and a good place for settling old scores without anybody to see.

Kapok will never go through Meiringspoort to Oudtshoorn. People like him have no courage for that, they stick to what they know, to roads they always travel. To cut through the Swartberg to a world of big towns and cars and white people would take guts he doesn't have. Besides, Meiringspoort is a tunnel that catches you between high peaks and the river. Even Kapok won't be that stupid – to take them into the mountains when they are running from a leopard who will keep after them long after all other hunters have given up.

Their fear floats on the air towards me and I laugh, watching them run. They are afraid of me. How do they know I am here? Something has spooked them. It is impossible. Nobody saw me. Why, when they were already resting, supposed to be settled for the night, did they pick up and take off? That's what is so irritating about karretjie-mense – they smell you, even when you are a mile away. They were calm until the boy came back from his wanderings. He came from the side of the farmhouse with something around his neck, a buck or a rabbit, which Kapok skinned and hung under the windmill. The boy put something in a bucket and pushed it under the seat of the cart. Everyone was resting. Then, all of a sudden, they all stood up, ins-panned the karretjie and were off.

Very funny, clever boy. You saw me on your walkabout. Spying on the spy. Watching me watching you. Then you edged around the farm, coming from the backside, knowing I was here on the koppie and I could see you. So you know I am here and you think you can outwit me. Yes. But next time, when I appear, you won't expect me. Next time you won't see me coming. In Leeu Gamka I was hungry for revenge and couldn't stop my rage. There I made mistakes. Now I will stalk you slowly, like you do the buck you love to eat. This time I will creep up close, with Jan's sharp blade ready, and I will cut my prey's throat when she least expects it. So long waiting and watching, my brother's life on her whore-hands, my son raised like a rat.

When the farmer and his dogs have settled for the night I'll short cut across the farm to the southern gate. Donkeys can't run forever.

28 MUIS

The whistle of the sjambok on the donkeys' backs is the song of the night. We run. On and on, until we see the opening through the mountains, and I pray this will be our escape. Miskiet will think we are too scared to go through the mountains. Meiringspoort is a tunnel to another world of big towns.

As the sky turns grey we walk into the Poort. The cliffs bend over us and block out the sky. We are in a twisting, turning tunnel now with rushing water under our feet. We could climb up its sides if we have to, but we won't get very far.

De Rust is on the other side and then, Kapok says, it is a morning's ride to Oudtshoorn. I have lived in the Great Karoo all my life but I have never been through Meiringspoort. You can see it, even from Leeu Gamka. When I first came to Leeu Gamka my eyes would follow the long black line of the Swartberg and then stop on the cut of God's only way through the great mountains.

Kapok says the donkeys need to rest but, when we stop, it is already too late.

"Whoa, whoa," his voice echoes from the tunnel's walls and the animals slow their gallop. He steers the karretjie off the road, on to a stony riverbank with reeds a little way off.

"We can hide here," he says. Then the karretjie falls forward as Pantoffel's legs fold under her.

"Get up, you stupid donkey. Staan op!" I scream from my seat on the karretjie. "Do you want him to kill me?"

Sponsie sits with big eyes on the karretjie bench. Witpop and Fansie's heads rise from the bak where they have been asleep.

Kapok jumps down and runs to Pantoffel, grabbing the harness on her head and trying to pull her back up, but she stays down.

"Nee, Pantoffel, op, op," he shouts. "Kom! Op, op." Fansie runs to help him and I see the boy bend to loosen the buckles keeping her in the karretjie.

Without the support of the harness and Rinnik, she lies flat on the riverbank, her sides heaving, her mouth and nose covered in foam, her hooves bleeding.

I am next to them now too, willing her up, but she stares at me, her empty animal eyes looking into mine. Then she closes them as if she is trying to shut me out.

"Please, Pantoffel, staan op," I say. But she lies, panting like a sick dog.

Fansie leads Rinnik into the reeds. Her back is raw from the night of whipping.

"We have run them too hard," Kapok says quietly. "Your fear has killed our donkeys."

"Your stupid donkeys." I lift my lip and spit the words at him. "Your stupid donkeys are useless."

I walk away, into the reeds behind the children, looking for a place where I can sit in peace and not see Pantoffel. The fear and anger in me swell up and I vomit into the sand, my throat on fire.

A little cold hand rests on my neck and Witpop kneels next to me.

"The water is sweet, Mamma, wet your face. Drink."

She leads me to a quiet place, out of sight of the road. I cup my hands in the water and take a few sips. I close my eyes and wet my face. Then without a word we both stand, our eyes searching for stokkies for a fire.

When I look up from the flames licking and chewing the wood, I see she and Fansie have the tin mug from the bag on the cart. They are pouring water over the cuts on Rinnik's back. Pantoffel is still lying where she fell, panting, but her breaths are slowing.

"There is aloe here in Meiringspoort. We must rub that on the donkeys' wounds," Kapok says.

He is on his knees beside Pantoffel, rubbing her all over with handfuls of sand. Afterwards he washes her bleeding body with water and squeezes aloe on her cuts.

"I have killed my donkeys, I have killed my donkeys," he mumbles.

I turn back to the fire where the coffee-pot boils.

Pantoffel has dropped by the road. Before the night is over we need to hide her and the karretjie. Kapok, Fansie and Witpop pull the karretjie into the water, pushing it up a far bank behind the reeds. It isn't a good hiding place but it can't be easily seen. Rinnik has lain down to sleep. Pantoffel hasn't moved.

"If Miskiet comes, he will see her," Kapok says. "We need to hide her away."

We cover her with reeds, so if someone passes they won't see it is a donkey, just a strange pile, like rubbish from the river.

If Miskiet finds us in Meiringspoort then, I know, it will be over. Here we can't hide our spoor. But if we can get through to Oudtshoorn, we will be safe. We must get to Home Affairs and get our papers. Then he will be afraid to kill me.

Before the sun rises we eat crabs that Fansie caught and which I drop into boiling water. I kill the fire and we go into the reeds to sleep. We will wait out the day and, when night comes, lead Rinnik into De Rust and try and sell her. The karretjie and Pantoffel will have to stay hidden until we can get back to them.

For a while we sleep. Kapok keeping watch, then me and then Fansie.

In the afternoon Fansie wakes us. "Look," he says.

Pantoffel has shrugged off her blanket of reeds and is up, making her way to us and Rinnik. She limps, but Kapok and Fansie meet her and lead her to the water where she walks in to drink.

We are rested and ready to move by dark. We hitch the donkeys again and I walk with the children, leading them out of the Poort. There has been no sign of Miskiet and although no one had spoken of him during the day, we know he is off our trail. We are going to Oudt-shoorn now and it will be easier to hide where there are more people.

Jan's face is in my mind now. His eyes that looked into mine and then at Miskiet before he fell into the dust with his brother's knife in his guts.

When I look at myself, my hard hands, torn and dirty clothes and starved stick legs, I can't understand Miskiet. Why does he want a useless, invisible woman? There are lots of fat and healthy town girls who will lie with him. Maybe he can't stand to think that I saw what he did. That every day it is in my head, same as it is in his. Maybe he wants to stop me from seeing. Or maybe all he wants is to teach me a lesson for not wanting him. He just wants to see me die.

29 WITPOP

This thing was lying in the road when we stopped, when Pantoffel fell, shining, even though the sun wasn't properly up. So I picked it up and let it slip in my sleeve before the others could see. I know it's a piece of mirror from a car and, if Fansie sees it, he will take it away from me and keep it. But it's mine. I found it so it's mine. Lucky for me he is helping Pappie try to make Pantoffel stand up. For once his jackal eyes aren't on me and he didn't jump on me when he saw me bend down and pick up my thing in the road. Its cold, sharp edge rubs my skin when we push the karretjie through the water and up the other bank. When I take Sponsie from Mamma I hold her with my other arm, careful, so it doesn't cut her. We look for stokkies, we pour water on Rinnik's cuts, we rub Pantoffel's legs, we drink coffee, we sit by the fire and my thing stays in my sleeve.

At last they sleep and Fansie climbs the bank on the other side of the road. I stand and watch him. He climbs higher and higher to a boesman cave. When he reaches the cave he disappears inside. I turn and walk along the river then slip behind reeds that hide me from the road. On the bank I sit flat and let the glass slip down my sleeve and on to the sand. They have mirrors in the toilets at the petrol station in Prince Albert. I looked in one there before the petrol-jokkie chased me outside again.

"Out, get out, we don't want you shitting all over our clean toilets."

Really, I wasn't going to mess – I just wanted to see my face. Now I have my own mirror and I hold it up to my eyes. It's only a small piece so I can't see my whole face. One black eye. Nose. Mouth full of sores. I look at them closely – some are bleeding with yellow crusts. If I hold my arms out straight then I can see my hair standing straight up. I bring it down and look at my feet, my toes touch the thing and I wiggle them. For a long time I look at my face again, blinking my eyes and feeling the hairs of my eyebrows.

"I am Witpop."

"This is Witpop." I see my lips make the words.

This is Witpop who is going to Oudtshoorn with her mamma and pappie and Fansie and Sponsie for identities. When we have identities we can get pay. Maybe then I should wait with the school shoes and rather get Vaseline for the sores on my mouth.

I lie down on the sandbank and let my hand play in the water.

The oom is chasing us because he is angry with Mamma about something that happened long ago.

We have to run to Oudtshoorn for identities or else he might catch us first. Mamma says that without identities we can be killed and nobody would look for us or miss us. Really, s'true. We have to exist for them to look for us and with no identities we don't exist.

We are running to Oudtshoorn and I am a stinking karretjiemeid. I stand up and pull my jersey and shirt over my head and throw them in the water, then I scrub them with sand. When I have them as clean as I can get them I lay them on a rock in the sun and start with my pants. I don't have underpants so it's just my long pants. Everything must go in the sun. At last I walk into the water. It's so cold the air comes out of me with a noise even though I am trying to be quiet. At the deepest part the water comes to the top of my legs so I go down and let it cover my shoulders. It's cold and I suck deep for air. I can see crabs playing wegkruipertjie under the rocks. There is a little red bird sitting on the reeds watching me. For a few moments I stay like that, then I go under. The cold is making my head sore. Under again and I pick up lumps of sand and start working it over my body. First my head and neck. Then more sand for under my arms. I rub my whole body, even my privates, with sand. It's not too bad and I become a fish. My skin is singing and I feel happy.

When I walk out I pretend I am a snake and I lie on the rock next to my clothes and let myself dry. It's so cold my teeth rattle in my mouth. My clothes are wet when I put them on again but I am clean all over. When we get to Oudtshoorn the children can tell me I am a karretjiemeid but I will not be a stinking one. I wrap my special thing in an old chip packet that I find near the road and put it in the wet pocket of my pants.

When I get back to the uitspan I see Pantoffel is standing up.

Fansie is back and he looks at me but says nothing. Pappie is so happy and Mamma is smiling. They don't notice I am wet and they don't notice I don't stink anymore.

30 KAPOK

What I want is a gun. It must be a small black gun, not one of those big long brown shotguns like the Boere use to kill rooikat. This gun must be easy to hide and it must have bullets inside. Ja, if I can get a gun I will feel much better. A knife is useful, but a person has to be very close for it to be any good. With a gun I can sit on the koppie and shoot. A gun will make us feel very safe.

For sure what I need is this small black gun. When we turn down a quiet road, when we sit around the fire, the shadow of this monster is there. Now each of us has an afraid look in our eyes as we wait for him to come. I know he is stalking us and we jump like bokkies at every rustle in the grass. Yes, I must get a gun because he won't expect me to have a gun.

Muis knew it would be like this even after all these years. "Anywhere, but not Leeu Gamka," she said. "It is a place with ghosts."

No Muis, not ghosts, it was the blerrie devil who waited for you. I didn't understand your fear. It was really the blerrie devil that kept you away all the time.

If I had a gun I could surprise him when he comes. I could take aim and pull the trigger and watch him fall, the same way a rooikat drops when a Boer shoots it with his big brown gun. Then I would leave him for the baboons and the jackals. Many years later someone might find a rib or his skull but by then it would be too late. No one would say, "But those karretjie people were in Meiringspoort that day, we must find them and ask them about this skull." We will move on, in our way, because we are invisible. No one would know it was Kapok with the donkey karretjie who pulled the trigger of a small black gun and killed the devil.

Miskiet wants to kill and that means when he comes no one will know he is here. We are running deeper into the crack in the mountains to hide from him. I didn't know which way to go. This way to Willowmore, that way to Prince Albert ... so I went straight. To blerrie Oudtshoorn. That is where she wants to go and, for once in her life, she is not moaning.

Now high mountains bend over, almost touching heads, as they watch us. This is not a good place to get caught. Only front or back. The sky has become small and the veld is gone. Our sky has always been big, our mountains, these mountains, were far away. Every road we went down, every turn, we knew where we were because the mountains showed us the way. Now, we are inside them and we are lost. I have heard that on the other side is De Rust and then Oudtshoorn. Places I have never been. Places my grandfather and then my father talked about by the fire of our uitspan. All my life I have heard of these places but I have never seen them.

It is in De Rust where I must get a gun. There will always be someone in the lokasie who wants to buy two donkeys and a karretjie and
there will always be someone who will want to sell a gun.

That is what I will do.

Fear has stolen Muis away. She does not talk but holds Sponsie
close to her, as if that will protect them both from the monster who is
chasing us. This life, this living in langkampe between fences at the
side of roads, is not for a little child. You know, we buried one, not long
ago, before Sponsie was born. Now when I see the hunger on Sponsie's
face my fear of Miskiet becomes small, it is Starvation that makes me
afraid. I don't want to bury a child again. When a child is hungry, long-
time hungry, its crying is not the angry screaming of a little one de-
manding to be fed. It is a strange cry, "hhaa hhaa", on and on for days.
Then one day it just stops and that is when you can know it has given
up. Then it looks at you with eyes that know Mamma and Pappie cannot make the pain go away. The little one who died, died from a fever,
but in my heart I know it was Starvation that took her. When I laid her
in the grave that the boy dug, her body was so light, just a few bones
covered in rags.

When I found work and Muis started eating properly again it was
kaboom! A blerrie baby coming again.

She didn't want Sponsie.

"How am I going to feed this child when you want to move up and
down the langkampe?" she shouted at me.

But what do you do when you get these tiny girl bundles? Mine are
always girls. Witpop, Meitjie and Sponsie. There have been no boys.

Fansie is my child because I took him for my own. He is my watch-
dog, creeping around our camp, sniffing the air, looking for signs of
something wrong. He is very good at tracking and I don't think Miskiet
will get close to us very easily with him here. Fansie will sniff his soap
on the night air the moment he is near. The boy is strong, watching out
for his old father with his bad leg, and his mother who is losing her
mind, and two useless sisters. What will he do when Miskiet comes?

He is tall and his chest is getting wider as he grows into a man, but he is so thin he could never fight a man who has eaten bread and meat every day for many years. It's just the look in his black eyes that makes me feel safe. That klonkie has the eyes of a clever young jackal. Jan's child.

Stupid little Witpop, gaaning aan about lappies and school shoes and pink roll-on. She lives in her world but now she is the only one there. Once she made us laugh with her dream of clothes and shiny shoes but those days are forgotten and now she rubs her hands and walks with her eyes down. I look at her and see a tiny child whose body is trying to become a woman but there is not enough flesh on her body for her to grow. Sores are klomped around her mouth and her knees stick out of her torn blue pants. When I look at her I know I must sell the karretjie and get a farm job where a farmer's wife can give her clothes and teach her letters and numbers.

But now, we are the sport of the blerrie devil.

Tonight we will carry on to De Rust and I will get a gun. When he comes I will shoot him. I will be ready.

The good news is that Pantoffel is up. Only Sponsie will ride so we can spare the donkeys. Muis has rubbed more aloe on the donkeys' cuts. With them looking so bad we won't get much. I am skaam for the whip marks on their backs. I am going to sell my donkeys. Yes, yes I must. The langkampe have so little for them to eat.

I am tired of donkeys. I am tired of their worms and their feet and their sores and their hunger. I am tired of the sjambok and of them falling down. Tomorrow, when they are sold, we can walk to blerrie Oudtshoorn and find that place that will give us identities.

31 FANSIE

This gun is small and heavy. They let me hold it in my hands and I turn it over and over, feeling its smooth cold surface. My fingers touch the tip and I wonder how many bullets have come screaming out of its little mouth. I hand it back to the shack-man and he takes it like someone who knows about guns, spinning it on a finger before wrapping it in a dirty white lappie and tucking it in his broek. The hok where we are sitting, the shack-man on a stool, Pappie on a red crate and me on a paint tin, is dark and smoky and my eyes are itching. I want Pappie to be finished with this gun buying so we can go outside.

"So it's R200?" Pappie asks for the third time. "That's your price, R200?"

The shack-man stands up.

"Okay. Okay!" Pappie wants the gun.

Coals burn red on a piece of sinkplaat on the floor and I cough. Jissie, there is no air in this place. Pappie feels for the brown notes wrapped in an old hankie and tucked in his shirt.

"Ha, boy, had enough of buying arms already?" The shack-man laughs. I can see his eyes in the dark and the flash of white teeth. We aren't buying arms, what does he mean? We are buying a gun to protect ourselves from a malletjie. The shack-man looks at me and chuckles.

"Come, ou man, make up your mind. I have other business today." This is a town man, he is not used to Pappie taking so long when he thinks about what he wants.

I keep my eyes down and I see bones scattered on the dirty cement floor. The shack people have sat around a pot on this fire and as they ate they threw the bones over their shoulders. The dogs haven't been in this morning to clean up.

This place where we are buying a gun is called Blomnek. Stem of a flower. How it got this name I don't know because there aren't flowers here and one with a stem wouldn't last. It's the lokasie for De Rust.

The white people live in De Rust and everybody else lives here. It's very early morning and outside children are crying and mothers are shouting.

Somebody called Benny doesn't want to go to school.

"Die fokken kind kort 'n pak!" There's the sound of a klap on skin and a child howls.

Dogs are barking at the boerebakkies coming and going as they fetch workers. Early morning, when the lokasie smells of mieliepap, we are buying arms.

"We'll take it," Pappie says eventually. "Are the bullets inside?"

The shack-man sighs. "It is fully loaded, yes." He takes the gun out and opens it again. I can see five small silver circles. "Just shoot, it'll work." He can see we know nothing of guns.

"Look here, ou man, this is the safety. You must pull it back before you shoot, you got it?"

Pappie nods his head up and down like Sponsie when Mamma gives her coffee and says she mustn't mess. When I look at the shack-man he is watching me and our eyes meet and we both smile at Pappie. Pappie is holding the gun saying, "The safety must come backwards, then I can shoot."

"That's right, you got it now ou man."

Pappie hands over the R200. Our donkey money. The man hands us the gun wrapped in its dirty lappie.

"Put it in your broek," Pappie says, giving it to me. Nobody will think a klonkie will be carrying a gun like this. It is difficult because I don't have an onderbroek, but I stick it in the waist of my pants and pull my jersey down. Pappie is so nervous he doesn't notice it's not properly in my broek. It pokes me but I feel important.

"Get rid of it when the job is done," the shack-man says. "Throw it in a deep river." At last we go outside and I take a breath of the morning air. Fresh in my lungs. The shack-man heads down the road with our donkey money in his hand.

Pappie and I walk down the hill back to Mamma and Sponsie and

Witpop who are sitting near the fast road to Oudtshoorn. Witpop has tied string around Rinkhals's neck to stop him from running in the road. All we have now is Rinkhals and three plastic packets, our pot and our blanket.

Pantoffel and Rinnik are gone and a terrible feeling comes over me. The donkeys and the karretjie are gone. Tears begin sliding down my cheeks and dripping on my jersey. I wipe my face on my sleeve but nobody notices. Pappie, Mamma, Witpop and Sponsie all have their heads down. We pick up our packets and our pot and our blanket and slowly we start the walk to Oudtshoorn.

32 WITPOP

The hills around De Rust are red, like blood, and I think that many people have died here to make them so. The donkeys are gone but I hear clip-clop, clip-clop behind me and keep looking back to see where they are. No. I shake my head. No donkeys. No karretjie. They are sold. Pappie says Pantoffel was going to die anyway, so it's better that somebody else has that problem.

We are on the other side of the Swartberg. When I look back at the mountains I can't believe there was a way through. On the other side are the vlaktes, with the roads and pathways we know so well. This side it is all farmland with goats and people. A person can't get lost here, there are too many people. Fansie is walking with me and while we walk tears run like flooding rivers over his cheeks but I pretend I don't see. I know why he is crying.

It's not lekker to see Fansie walking when he always runs. Is he going to slow down forever, now that Pantoffel and Rinnik and the karretjie are gone?

Really, what are we going to do? When we go back will we still walk in the veld but with no donkeys and karretjie?

"Sss, Sss."

I am thinking and I don't hear him straight away.

"Sss, Sss."

Fansie makes a movement with his head for me to fall back and walk with him.

Far in front of us Mamma has Sponsie on her back and Pappie is just behind her, carrying the pot and the blanket. We slide into a ditch by the road and sit for a little while. Then he talks. He talks to me like a sister, not a shouting talk but a real talk, and I nod. I understand.

When we are back on the road we run to catch up. Mamma and Pappie's heads are still down. They didn't see we were gone.

Now I walk with my head up and my shoulders back. I am not a dom meid. Now I am an important sister with a big job to do for my brother. I am not afraid, I am brave and I am clever.

All day we walk. When it's nearly dark I see the lights. First it is a long star-snake twinkling far away. I can't take my eyes off it and I stumble over rocks by the road. Once I nearly fall down a steep bank next to the road. "There is Oudtshoorn," Pappie shouts back to us.

For the first time I hear hope in his voice. There is Oudtshoorn where we will get identities. And, please, some food.

My stomach is squeezing and turning, telling me it wants to eat. We did eat a little today. A big fat policeman sitting by the road gave us his bread and polony. He was a nice man to do that. If he didn't give us that bread and polony I would have stopped walking long ago. Now it is getting dark. I am afraid and I run to be with Mamma. Pappie waits for me so that we can walk into Oudtshoorn together.

There are lots of cars now and their lights are shining in my eyes.

"They are town people," Pappie says. "They need cars to get around."

"Mamma?"

She doesn't look up and the sound of my voice hangs in the air.

101

I want to say, "Mamma, I am tired and I am hungry." I want to ask her, "Mamma, can we stop now and make camp here?" In the end I say nothing. One foot in front of the other. My head down now so the cars' lights don't hurt my eyes. Walking under the snake lights. I wonder if we could get a car if we lived in a town. We don't need donkeys and a karretjie if we have a car. Fansie and I could crawl underneath at night to sleep and Mamma and Sponsie could sleep inside. Pappie knows how to drive donkeys. I am sure he could drive a car.

The star-snake is made of streetlights. From far away you couldn't see it was lights on poles, just a silver snake sliding into the sky.

How do they do that? How do they get a light on the top of a pole?

Streetlights make it easy to see, even in the dark, and I watch the faces of people standing around. They look at us as if we are wild animals that have come out of the dark.

Mamma in her brown rags with a baby tied to her back. Pappie limping after the long walk today. And me. Me. Barefoot in boy's pants and a jersey full of holes, my hair sticking up like grass and the sores all over my mouth. Again I hear clip-clop, clip-clop and I look back for Fansie and the donkeys but there is nothing there. And then I see that Fansie has gone.

33 KAPOK

Blerrie Oudtshoorn. Shoo ... My leg thumps like a knife is being pushed into it all the time. We don't talk anymore. We just walk. On and on and on. This afternoon we passed the road to Dysselsdorp and I said to Muis we should rest under a tree for a while.

There was a nice tree not very far up the road but when we came closer I saw there was a speed cop sitting in the shade, taking pictures of cars that went too fast. We sat under a tree nearby and watched him for a while. This speed cop was very fat. When he had a fast one and he wanted to take a picture, he leaned forward quickly. His stomach hung over his pants and, between the buttons of his shirt, his hairy skin peeped out. He didn't talk to us but just worried about taking pictures.

I liked watching him and I waited for a car to see if he was going to take a picture. Soon I could hear if a car was coming too fast and I thought, "Oohh, you are going to get a photograph."

After a while Muis stood up and tied Sponsie on to her back. First a knot on her chest and then another on her stomach. She started walking again without talking.

I reached out my hands to Witpop and she pulled me up. When I looked at the traffic cop for the last time, he was watching us, but quickly he leaned forward into his camera when a car flashed past.

As we moved the traffic cop shouted, "Hey!"

I was so on my nerves that I did a little jump.

"Ja, Meneer?" I called back to him.

He pointed at Witpop and waved a paper packet at us.

"Gaan, gaan," I said to her.

I gave her a push.

She walked towards him, unsure what he wanted. He gave her the packet and smiled.

Witpop took the packet without a word.

Inside was polony and a stukkie brood.

When I looked at the traffic cop to smile and wave he was leaning forward again to take a picture. He had already forgotten us. Muis was far ahead but Witpop ran to catch up with her and I saw her breaking off pieces of the bread and pushing them into Sponsie's mouth.

On and on. The grey backs of Pantoffel and Rinnik come into my mind. My hands move reins that are not there. Pantoffel came with the karretjie so many years ago I can't remember. There was a pony too, but he died. Donkeys do better in the langkampe. They have

103

sharper teeth to eat the bossies. Rinnik was Pantoffel's foal who used to run next to the karretjie. When the pony died I put her in next to her mother. Those blerrie donkeys. "Dié kant!" and they would go this way, "dáái kant" and they would go that way. I bought the karretjie, the pony and Pantoffel from Oom Chrisjan at Rietbron for R50. That was before Fansie was born, before I knew Muis and when Mina and I rode through the Karoo.

Pantoffel came a long way with me and in the end I beat her until she fell down and then I sold her for a gun.

When we had food, that donkey would lick out the pot like a dog. Muis would laugh and say, "Pantoffel, you are the only donkey in the Karoo that eats meat."

I think that donkey was just hungry, the dry grass of the langkampe isn't always enough to keep a donkey going.

By night the lights of Oudtshoorn are clear. We are here. As we walk into town I feel excited. Today we have passed a difficult test. All that I worry about now is that Fansie has not come back. Fansie and Pantoffel's gun.

For a while we stand on a street corner not sure where to go until a woman asks Muis "Wat soek jy?"

"That place where you get identities," Muis says.

"Ah, that's not difficult," the woman answers. "Turn down here and walk straight and when you get to the bottom turn and walk up the hill, that way." She points and smiles. "And this child," she asks. "This child has been carried a long way?" She touches Sponsie's cheek and presses a R5 into Muis's hand. "Buy her some milk." Then she walks on and, in the dark, we go the way she pointed to the place where you get identities.

34 MISKIET

They are spread out, walking very slowly. I was lucky. A bakkie picked me up when I reached De Rust and then it was caught behind a truck just when we passed them. All they could see was a labourer on his way to the farm for another day behind a shovel. A grey blanket pulled over his head. Hidden. One, two, ah, Kapok, three. Dragging behind, limping. She is far ahead, not looking back, not waiting, not caring. The girl is between them, barefoot. Once the girl turned to look for Kapok but he was too slow and she carried on before he caught up. The boy has gone again. Useful to have a quick boy like that to send around when you have a limping leg and want food.

They never saw me. They didn't notice a man with a blanket pulled over his head on the back of a bakkie. Their heads were down, aiming for Oudtshoorn.

I never thought they would go through the Swartberg and now I am excited that they chose this way. I followed their spoor and when I came to the tar road I went to Klaarstroom and then a little way to Prince Albert, but I could soon see no donkeys went that way. Then on the Willowmore road there were no tracks. So, mense, you chose the mountains, eh? Braver than I thought. If I could have caught them there it would have been good but I wasted time looking up and down the side roads. But that's no problem. They don't know which way to go in the town. The crowds and the traffic will confuse them. I will get her there.

Yes, Muis. Every step of this journey is one you chose.

Tonight you will have a visitor again. Tonight this visitor will finish what he started.

The bakkie overtook a truck and they disappeared. I wanted to get off at once and wait for her. I could hide behind a tree then step out as she walked past.

"*Ja, Muis. Now we can have some fun.*"

"*No, please Miskiet, I am sorry.*"

"*Sorry? It's too late for sorry. You are a hoer.*"

Even though I am on the bakkie I open Jan's knife and I stab the air. I feel the pleasure of plunging it into her guts and pulling it out so that it makes a wet sucking noise and she tries to breathe in and that is wet too. I have to fight with myself to stay down and not to jump off the moving bakkie.

Sit, Miskiet, sit. Patience. Wait. Be still like a cat watching a nest of mice.

Then the warm feeling is gone and rage floods into me, making my head feel like it is going to explode.

Close eyes, head down. In my pocket I find my Disprins and I take two to suck.

That filthy, scrawny chicken, who should be scratching around the backyards of a lokasie, turned her back on me. She, a nothing, walked away from me with the son I wanted.

You come to us you and you look at me with hot eyes and I can see you thinking I am a mooi outjie. I see you licking your lips when I am near and checking me out when you think I'm not watching. You spy on me through the back window when I am washing. I see everything. But then one day it's Jan buying you cooldrink and Jan who you wait for at the tunnel and Jan lying with you on the floor on the other side of the curtain.

She trapped my brother and, because of her, he had to die.

Tonight her witch's blood will soak into the ground of their dirty Oudtshoorn camp.

You have run all this way, Muisie, and when you get to Oudtshoorn, I will be waiting for you.

35 FANSIE

Before today I never touched a gun. This one is small and black with brown on the handle and it is heavy. While they were walking I climbed down a bank next to the road to have a good look at it. I put my eye over the little hole on the end but I couldn't see anything. That's where the bullets come out. It smelt like matches.

"Pow!"

For a while I let my finger rest on the place where you shoot. I could kill something if I wanted to. There was a bird in the grass, hopping around catching goggas.

"Die bird," I said, and I pointed the gun.

"Boom." The bird heard me and flew away. There were sheep in a field in front of me and I took shots at them.

"Boom, boom, boom." They never lifted their heads, just carried on eating. This small, smooth thing kills people. At first I didn't want to touch it. It was like touching a snake and I thought it would spin around and strike. But now that I have had a good look at it I can see it's only a thing. For the first time in my life I feel like I am the baas with a skivvie.

Be careful of me for I have a gun.

Respect me for I have a gun.

Now I understand why the Boere like their guns so much. A gun makes you feel like you can boss people. The Boere have much bigger guns than mine, long guns. Shotguns. Now, when I sit and think about it, I am not jealous because in the end, it's the same. This gun can also kill.

When we were staying at the farm Hartseerbos, Meneer Kobus used his long gun to shoot the cats on the farm. One night he had no sleep because the cats were "maauu, maauu, maauu" outside his window. We heard his wife, Mevrou, try and chase them by spraying water with the hose pipe in the middle of the night.

"Voetsak!" she shouted.

"Weg is julle!"

"Shoo, shoo."

The next day Meneer Kobus told Pappie and the other workers to catch all the cats on the farm and put them in feed bags. Some bags had five cats. Then he shot up all the bags with his long brown gun. Boom, boom, boom. He stopped to put bullets in his gun then carried on. As each bag stopped wriggling and blood dripped through on to the dust, Pappie's job was to take it away and burn it. Pappie made a big fire with old car tyres and a long black cloud hung in the blue sky. The air was thick with that smoke and it made all the children cough and choke. Pappie never opened the bags, he just threw them on the big fire while Meneer Kobus carried on shooting.

"Sss, sss," I stood up and called Witpop. "Come sit with me for a while."

We both held the gun and I let her smell its little mouth.

"It does smell like matches," she said.

Before we stood up I tied the gun to her belly, tight, with a long piece of tou I found in the road. I threaded it through the handle around her middle and back again, then I tied a knot. When she runs, it won't drop out.

I showed her the safety and how to be sure it stayed on so the gun didn't shoot by itself.

As we walk and Oudtshoorn comes closer, my mouth feels dry and my hands sweat. She has our donkey-gun and now I can go. Pappie didn't want to carry it. He looked at it but he wouldn't touch it.

36 MUIS

We are here. The walking wasn't so bad. It is Sponsie who is hurting my heart. No crying anymore, just half noises that I have heard before. Hunger crying. Fansie has gone but I know he is looking for food. He will come and he will bring us something to eat.

"Fansie is coming, Sponsie. Sshh, sshh. Fansie is coming with food for you. Net nou, net nou."

Her little head rests between my shoulders and I hear her hunger-cry again.

Miskiet has not shown his face again. As we walked I thought about what I did wrong. Long ago, when my brother dropped me at the cross-roads on the N1 with Pappa's donkey karretjie, I did not want a boyfriend. It was food and a place to sleep that I needed, and to get away from Pappa's hidings. If I could live quietly, in a hok, out of the way. Maybe find a domestic job or picking up rocks for the roads' people.

I am sorry I made Miskiet angry. I am sorry he killed Jan. I am sorry I ran away with Kapok. That's me, always scared, always running away from hidings. I am sorry my children are hungry. As I walk I cry for all the things I did wrong.

"Oh Here, Liewe Jesus, help my asseblief."

I am a nothing person but my heart feels like it is as big as the whole world and it is breaking into small pieces. On and on we walk and, as I walk, each one talks to me. Fansie, Sponsie, Witpop and Meitjie.

"Mamma, who is my father?"

"I am hungry."

"Can I also go to school?"

"I am cold."

My children. I want to give these things to you but the veld is our only father. He will feed us and teach us and shelter us. Sometimes this father wants to give us hidings and make us sorry.

Oudtshoorn comes slowly in the first dark of the night. First shacks, then new government houses and then people. On a street corner I stop, not knowing where to go. A woman in smart clothes, maybe a sister from the clinic, sees me looking around and she tells me how to get to the place for identities.

"Down this hill and through the lokasie," she says, pointing with her whole arm. "Turn at the bottom and go up, you must go up again, past the ostrich abattoir. You will know it's the abattoir because it stinks." She wrinkles her nose like she is smelling the old blood right then. "The small green building with a high fence is Home Affairs," she says. "That is the place where you can sort out your ID books."

Before she spoke I had watched her coming down the road. She looked like she was going home, a town lady, with a good job. Heavy shopping bags were cutting into her hands. Her head was down, like she was very tired and she was thinking about something important. Then, as she was about to cross the road, she looked up and saw me standing on the corner. I turned away so she wouldn't think I had been watching her and I went and stood by the fence of a big building. I didn't mean to look at her; it was only because I didn't know where to go. She crossed the road and walked towards me and I felt my heart start running. Is she going to klap me? Can you klap a person for looking?

"Where do you come from, mommy?"

The working town lady is talking to me.

I say nothing. She waits for my answer, and, at last, my invisible voice comes and I whisper, "Anderkant die berge, suster."

"Did you walk from the other side of the mountains?" Her voice is strong like she knows the answer already.

I nod.

"Why are you here? In this place, hey? This is not your place."

"We are coming for identities."

"You want an ID book?"

I can hear she is used to asking dom people like me questions.

I nod again. That's when she tells us where to go.

"It's very easy," she says.

When she sees I understand she scratches in her handbag for cents but finds a R5 and pushes the shiny coin into my hand.

"Buy your child some milk," she says.

When I raise my eyes to say thank you she is looking at me. Then she shakes her head and turns away.

"Dankie, suster," my voice comes out louder now and she stops again and turns to me.

"Good luck, mommy."

Then she carries on down the road with her packets. Kapok and Witpop are standing in the shadows but they come now to hear what the woman said. We rest then I pick up Sponsie, tie her to my back and we walk down the road, the way the woman said we should go.

When we pass a huiswinkel Kapok goes inside and buys half a loaf of white bread with the R5. I give Sponsie a little piece and she lifts it to her mouth. Witpop eats and Kapok and I share the rest. Fansie will bring more food.

In the dark we find Home Affairs. It is easy to see the green walls because of the streetlights.

"We will come back very early tomorrow," says Kapok, "before they open the doors. We will be first."

We walk down the hill behind the Home Affairs building looking for a quiet place to sleep and then, we are very lucky, we find the river. Kapok and Witpop pick up stokkies for a fire and, at last, I can lie down with Sponsie and sleep.

37 FANSIE

Doors hang open but people don't see me. I watch and wait. Jissie, these town people are easy prey, slow rabbits. Town people don't notice change around them. They don't hear me kick a stone or sniff or cough. Even tortoises are cleverer than these people, and this makes me laugh. A slow tortoise knows: keep still, say nothing and nobody will see you.

Rinkhals once sniffed out a puff adder. I would never have known it was there, curled by a rock next to the path, until it moved. When that snake saw me it made as if to be dead and it disappeared again. My foot would have come down right next to it and I wouldn't have seen it. I poked it with a stick and it did nothing. Then, as I looked around for a rock to klap it, it flew up and went for the stick. I jumped back and screamed, laughing. Jissie that was a slim slang! After that I thought about that snake for a long time and then I knew. If you are still, not talking and not moving, people don't see you. I tried it out in the veld and it worked. I can catch a dove with my hands. It is easy. I lie still, somewhere near water, and think I am a puff adder. A puff adder that has its whole life to catch one bird. Kurr, kurr, kurr. I listen to the doves talking. Be a puff adder. Bly stil, bly stil. Then in one move I grab it. In my hands I have its tiny brown body with scared black eyes. Birds are so small and soft that if I squeeze too tight I crush their ribs. Sometimes I eat the birds I catch, but most days I let them fly away because they teach me that, if I lie still, I can catch them.

In this place, this Oudtshoorn lokasie, it is easy to find food, much easier than catching birds. I watch an aunty making bread. Flour is mixed with water and a little bit of yeast. Then the lump of dough is put under a lappie to rise in the sun. I could take the dough for Mamma but I leave it to see how the aunty's bread will come out and if it will taste better than bread cooked on a fire. Later she comes back and tests the dough with her finger. Nice and puffy, just right for baking. She carries it inside, and through her open door I see her pressing it into the baking pans. She opens the stove and pushes the bread pans in. It is a town stove, like the stove at the Seekoegat school. This stove is against the wall and is not a wood stove like the stoves in some farmhouses. Mamma makes our bread on the coals, little roosterkoekies that she turns quickly to stop them burning. They taste best very hot and dipped in coffee. The aunty will have to cut her bread with a knife, into slices, like in a shop. Our knife won't cut it properly so I think we will break it into pieces. With the bread in the stove, the aunty goes next door to talk to her friend, a dik ou tannie. They sit outside drinking coffee and the aunty's friend tightens the curlers in the aunty's hair.

After a while, she comes back and takes the bread out and turns it upside down on the table to take it out the pans. My jackal nose sniffs the air and my jackal stomach starts biting me to tell me it is very hungry. I move around the houses, away from the bread, and then back, through the backyard shacks, behind the aunty's house again. The radio is on, playing Gospel.

"Jesus, Liewe Jesus, oooohh, Here ..."

"Grieta, come listen," the aunty shouts from the door. Her friend is now washing clothes in a bak on top of a black rubbish bin.

"Nee man, come this side," Grieta shouts back. "Bring the radio so Oupa can listen too."

An old, old oupa is sitting outside the door, on a red crate with a stick next to him. It looks like he is blind. I must be careful of him. My cousin Kobus's oupa is blind and he sees me before anyone else. Blind people are the only ones who are awake in a town.

"Blerrie Grieta, now I must unplug the radio," the aunty says to herself. She walks back to Grieta's place with the radio and its cable and they go inside to plug it in. I slip into her kitchen. There is nobody in the house. It is one big room with curtains blocking off the sleeping place. This is a rich aunty. She has lots of things pushed into her house, even a TV.

The bread is hot so I wrap it in the lappie she left on the table. There are two loaves but I leave one for the aunty because I don't want her children to be hungry like me.

Where is she? I look carefully out the door and I can't see her but I hear her talking to the dik aunty, Grieta, about what music must be on the radio. I slide out the door and walk quickly around the back of her house and between the shacks, and then I run.

Ek het brood, groot, mooi, warm brood. Spit is running out my mouth, my nose is running and my stomach is crying and shouting, "Gee my brood, gee my brood."

I don't want to eat it yet. I want to bite and smell it and hug its hot body. But I know people will see I am hungry and they will know this is stolen bread. So I run downhill with the bread wrapped in its lappie. I run all the way to the reeds because I know there is a river. That is where my family will be. They will be very hungry and very happy to eat this beautiful bread.

38   MISKIET

The bakkie stops by a fruit tent where Somalis are selling naartjies, so I jump off. I can see the place where I will wait. The fruit tent is at the entrance to a cemetery where rows of graves cover a hillside. I walk through a fancy gateway that has no gates and no fence on either side. That is lucky. Nobody cares who comes and goes; this is a good place to wait.

Small heaps of hard red dirt show where bodies are buried. Only some have headstones and everywhere there is broken glass from smashed jam-jar vases. All these dead people buried in this dry place with rubbish on top of them.

You know something, Klein Muisie? You are not going to have one of these glass-sprinkled red heaps. When I am finished with you I am going to throw you away, like a piece of rubbish.

The Somalis sell me a bag of naartjies for R5. I am very hungry now and trek up the hill between the graves, looking for somewhere to sit where I can eat. Nobody looks my way. Nobody cares about a man in a blue overall with a packet of naartjies and his head down. From the top of the cemetery I can watch the road. Leaning against a big headstone I sit down to wait. From this spot I will see them coming and which way they will go. It is late now, and the way they are walking, they will come with the dark, but I will see them, little people lit by streetlights.

This is a good place to sit.

To pass the time I take out my new knife, Jan's knife, and scrape the blade on the headstone until it is sharper than ever. My old knife, the one they stole, had cut the throats of many sheep, it had slaughtered plenty of pigs, it had shut up one of Ting-a-Ling's yapping dogs and it had killed Jan.

This new knife has done nothing yet, but now it will stop you, Klein Muisie, for being disrespectful.

When I think how you made me suffer, I burn inside. Then a picture of me kicking you comes into my mind and it feels like water being poured on a fire. I want to hear you scream. You can beg me to stop but, this time, I am going to sort you out. First you are going to get a few klaps and then you are going to beg for your life. Like I should have made you do all those years ago.

I plunge the tip of my new knife tip into a naartjie and look at it. It is a good knife, a killing knife.

I want you, even in your laprok and frayed doek, but you think you are too good for me. You have no manners. You go to Jan instead. I know what the two of you are doing. I hear your giggling and whispering on the kitchen floor. If I make a sound, or turn in my bed, you go quiet.

One time, when we are alone, I touch your back with my flat hand, a soft touch, to show you I care, that I also want to whisper in your ear. You go stiff, like wood, and your mouth curls down.

You people live in my house, but you have no respect. It should be Jan listening to the fast breathing on the other side of the thin curtain during the night.

Now I want this thing to be over. Even though I am sitting quietly, my face and body are wet and drops of sweat are falling into the dirt. I put my hand on my heart to slow it down.

I want you to be dead, Muis. Today you will beg me for mercy and I will laugh at you. It will be over and then, after all these years, I can be free.

The best way to gut a sheep, after its throat has been cut, is to hold the knife in your fist and cut backwards. The knife must be sharp. When you slaughter a pig it's important to plunge the knife straight into its heart so it dies immediately. A pig screams when it dies and the person who is doing the slaughtering must block his ears to the terror. I don't mind killing a pig – it can scream its head off and I plunge the knife straight in. To end a person's life slowly, the knife must go into the stomach. That way you can have a conversation and explain things as the person bleeds to death. But tonight I am not in the mood for talking; tonight it will be a cut throat with spraying blood, over and done. She will know why. She doesn't need any talking.

Your time has come, Muis, and tonight I will be merciful and let you die quickly. All I want is for you to understand that you will die and that I will take the child that is mine.

As the day becomes night, I see her. The shape I have been waiting for all these years. Head down, child tied to her back.

What do you want in Oudtshoorn, Klein Muisie?

It was a wasted walk, Klein Muisie.

All this way for nothing.

Kapok and the girl have caught up and are a few steps behind her. Where is the boy? He is still not with them. They want to make camp now; they'll need water. For a long time they stand on a street corner not knowing where to go. A woman gives them directions and they move off down the hill, towards the river. It is time to go. I stand up, wipe my knife with my hankie, snap it shut and slip it into place.

It is dark when I find them at the river. The girl has been picking up stokkies and papers and she gets a fire going. They have nothing to eat and the boy should have come back with food by now. I want him to come so that I can explain things to him. He will understand because he is my son. They are waiting for him too. The fire dies down and the night goes quiet. Lights in the windows of houses go out and I stand up and move closer.

When I walk into their camp, they look up at me, woken from a hungry sleep.

"Hullo, Klein Muisie."

She staggers to her feet. The dog is barking but they have tied him to an old tyre and he can do nothing. Kapok feels around in the dark for his knobkerrie. Ah, no chance of that again. It is there, resting on a rock by the dying coals, and I pick it up and throw it into the reeds. It's easy this time. I walk around the fire, stepping over the sleeping baby.

"Build up the fire, girl," I say.

She heaps stokkies and papers in the circle of stones and puts a match to it. The flame eats the wood and a circle of light shines on their scared faces. Even the baby is sitting up now, watching me.

I laugh. "You are mine, Klein Muisie. I decide what happens. You should have listened."

In the end it is so easy. After all her years of running and hiding I can touch her. In the beginning it would have been gentle, but now I grab her shirt and pull her to her feet.

My blade is at her throat. Little drops of blood appear like red beads on a necklace.

"Hold still and come with me," I whisper in her ear.

I drag her, but even though she is so thin, she makes her knees fold and her body goes pap. Heavy.

"Walk properly." I push my knee hard into her back and she sucks in air but says nothing.

It is then the boy comes, out of the dark, with bread in his hands.

"Good boy," I say, "you can make us food."

117

He looks at me with blank black eyes, no fear on his face.

"You are my son," I tell him, pressing the knife to his mother's throat a little harder. "She took you away from me. Hey Muis? " Her black eyes look at me and I can feel her shaking.

"Ja Muis? Hey? Tell the boy how you let me become a father and why you have run away from me all this time."

Ah, blood. A drop of blood runs out her nose and into her mouth. There is going to be more of that now.

We stand still, watching each other. My knife is at her throat, the boy holds the food. Kapok stays sitting on the ground, useless without his stick.

Then, in the dim light, there is a movement on the edge of the circle of light and I see it is the girl. In her hands she has a gun.

"Nee, girlie," I say.

Her eyes are big and wild but I am not afraid of her.

"Give me the gun."

39   FANSIE

This morning I saw some boys take an oompie's money out of his pockets, just like that. Jissie, he wasn't passed out, but he was very drunk and he tried to fight with them but they just went through his pockets quickly, took his money and left him sitting on his bum in the street, vloeking. They just laughed at him.

When I found a dronkie I did the same. The oompie I chose was at the side of a road, snorking lekker. I knew he was going to buy more wine when he stood up so it was better that I had his money. I found a tiny pink R50 rolled into a ball, wrapped in a piece of newspaper, inside his pants pocket, under his overall. He thought it would be hidden from thieves there but I found it. That's a lot of money. We can buy sugar and flour and coffee for R50.

It was good I learnt what those boys do to get money. Now if I find someone lying so drunk they can't stand up, I am going to take all the money out of their pockets. A dronkie lying in the road deserves to have no money. When Pappie is drunk I look after him. I take his money and give it back in the morning and he and Mamma laugh.

"Ja, my seun. I would have been robbed if it wasn't for you."

Mamma never has money in her pockets. Maybe a packet of tobacco or matches, but that is all.

Tonight they will make camp near the high riete that are good for hiding. The easiest way is down the busy road in the middle of the houses. I play that I am a child, running home with Mamma's shopping. I dream she is waiting for me with a bowl of curried afval. Mmm, my mouth is watering. It's just what I feel like eating. It's getting dark now and I want to break a piece off the brood.

"Leave it, Fansie," I say in a cross voice like Mamma. "Mamma must have the whole beautiful and full brood. You can't give her half a brood."

For a long, long time I walk along the river, between old paint tins and broken bottles, looking for their camp. A cat runs between the riete and hides. Two dogs are eating out of a packet and they bark at me but I pretend they aren't there and they go back to their eating. Stars are starting to twinkle and I stop and look up to find Meitjie's star. It's always the brightest and it's always in the sky.

Hullo Meitjie, where are you tonight?

The air is full of wood smoke so I can't sniff them out. I want to cry. I am hungry and I don't know this place. I want to see Pantoffel and Rinnik and feel their ears and their backs.

Let your ears hear, Fansie. Shouting voices, barking dogs, running water, cars, crying. I am still too close to town, so I walk on.

Where are you, Mamma?

Riete sway in the night breeze. Now I hear a night bird call. Feel them. I look for the yellow from their fire. And then, at last, I see it and I hear Rinkhals barking. He is barking like a mal hond, and then I know something is wrong and I run. When I am close, I see everything. That oom is there and he is holding Mamma with his blade at her throat. Sponsie is sitting, looking up at Mamma.

"Los, los," she is saying and her little arms are reaching up, but Mamma can't pick her up because the oom is holding her and a knife is cutting into her. He has another one, the same as before. How can he have two of the same? Pappie is half sitting, half lying. He can't get up. Mamma sees me and her voice is a cry. "Fansie."

Everyone is quiet and one word, my name, floats up like smoke on the night air.

I want to shout, "I have come, Mamma, and I have a beautiful brood and money for you."

Witpop is by the fire where she has made a heap of stokkies. Now her wild eyes look into mine. Without a sound, while Mamma and the oom are watching me, Witpop stands up and walks off into the dark, like she always does, like I taught her, when there is trouble.

Hide Witpop, keep your body still. Don't make a sound and they will never find you.

That's what I taught her to do when they are drinking and the fighting starts.

Sponsie has gone to Pappie now and he holds her, telling her, "Bly stil, bly stil."

The oom looks at me and smiles so that his teeth show and even in the dark I see the glint of the stone in his front tooth that he wears to make him look like a rich man.

Everything is quiet now, even Rinkhals. And then Mamma starts to cry.

He is holding her shirt but he kicks her to shuddup and she screams in pain.

"Don't hurt my mamma, Oom," I say in a strong, cross voice. He looks at me and smiles.

Behind him, the moon is rising, a big yellow ball, like a night sun in the black sky. We look at each other, him smiling and me watching his face, waiting for it to change, waiting for him to slice through Mamma's throat. I must jump then, I must kick and hit and bite.

His eyes shift and I turn. Witpop is back, standing on the other side of the fire, both arms straight out in front of her with Pantoffel's gun between her hands, pointing at him and Mamma. Sweat shines on her face. Her eyes are strange and black and she stares straight at him. One finger is on the trigger and I wonder how she knows what to do and if she can shoot.

That gun. I didn't want to take it when I was looking for food. If I was caught with a gun, it would have been taken off me. It is our donkey-gun, it is all we have. The oom laughs quietly and lifts the knife from Mamma's throat and lets her go. She slides to the ground and lies at his feet, too scared to move but watching Witpop with wide eyes.

"Give me the gun, girlie." His smile is a begging smile and he reaches out to Witpop with the knife still in his hand.

"You don't want to kill anyone. That thing is very dangerous."

Her hands are shaking but her fingers tighten and she keeps her grip. Pappie and Sponsie stay sitting on the ground by the fire. Sponsie is quiet, watching Witpop. Mamma lies at the oom's feet, like a sack of flour. Then, before my ears are sure what they have heard, there is a growl, like a rooikat in a vanghok. An angry, wild sound that makes you step back. It takes a second before I realise it is Witpop. I don't know if she is starting to cry. The oom hears it too and he steps towards her. A drop of sweat slides from her face.

Then he speaks: "We are family, girlie, I am Fansie's father." He takes another step and reaches his empty hand out for the gun.

"You can't shoot, girlie."

40 KAPOK

When it comes it's not what I expected. I feel the change in her before she moves. Jislaaik. Just a small twitch and her finger closes.

The shot cracks the air like a sjambok. My ears ring and then I hear people shouting. Miskiet looks at her with surprise and smiles again. There is blood on his shirt. Then he goes down slowly, on to his knees and on to his side with the knife in his hand. On the ground he turns and looks at Fansie and tries to speak but all that comes is a borreling. We watch him, nobody moves. The shouting up on the road is getting more and more.

Then me and Fansie move together. Fansie fetches my knobkerrie from the riete where Miskiet threw it and pulls me on to my feet. Jinne tog. Wat het nou gebeur? Jissus. I stamp out the fire and push Sponsie to Muis, who is still on the ground.

Fansie takes the gun from Witpop's hands while I push Miskiet on to his back. Spit and blood run from the corner of his still-smiling mouth, the tooth with the stone shines in the moonlight. His eyes, soos blerrie moddergate, look into nowhere and I know he is dead for sure this time.

"Check him for money, Fansie."

The boy gives me Pantoffel's gun and I kapok-run to the edge of the riete and throw it as far as I can. With one little splash it is gone.

"Hier's R500 in sy sak, Pappie."

"Give it to me."

Fansie uncurls Miskiet's fingers from the knife. Muis's blood has made a thin line on the blade and he rubs it one, two in the sand, wipes it with a piece of Witpop's fire paper, snaps it closed and slips it in his pocket.

"I want one of those knives, hey," I tell him. "You've got two now." He smiles.

"Come this side, Fansie." We drag the body to the riete and then into the cold black water. It's shallow when we start, but as we walk it gets deeper and we keep going, pulling the body between us. When it is up to our middles we let it go.

"No one will find him here. What's left of him will wash away with the next flood."

We push through the riete to the bank.

"Kom julle," I tell them. "We must move now before the people come."

Fansie spreads the ashes from the fire and brushes away our tracks. Muis is up, picking up our things, ready to move. I pick up Sponsie and take Witpop by the hand. Rinkhals sniffs the blood in the sand then turns away and trots ahead.

High up on the hill I see the blue lights of a police car coming down the road to the river. They are looking to see where the shot was fired, they are looking for the gun and what it has done. People are shouting, dogs are barking.

In the dark we move along the river bank, away from the voices. After a long time we cross the main road to George and rest under the bridge. Muis and Witpop haven't talked. Fansie makes a small fire and boils coffee, then we break up his stolen bread and eat. We are wet but there is no time for drying clothes now.

41   MR HENDRIKS

They are at the gate when I round the corner in my car. Their black, expressionless eyes watch me when I unlock the padlock on the gate but I ignore them. Today I am early. Today I will be one step ahead of the rows of idiots waiting for help, including this lot.

"God grant me patience," I say out loud.

What will the next eight hours bring? Rude whites wanting instant passports, fourteen-year-old girls registering newborns so they can claim welfare grants, septic-looking identity documents that I wouldn't touch with a pair of tweezers but which I have to open to see the grime-smeared youthful face of the old man waiting in line.

Once I have parked, in the shade of the only tree, I see they have followed me in and are waiting in a corner near the gate. Father, mother and three children, all bloody starving, that much is obvious. They look dishevelled, first time in town from the Great Karoo, I guess, and probably not a flaming official paper between them.

Oh, for the love of Nelson Mandela, give me patience today.

I let myself in through the red door of the prefabricated building and close it. Home Affairs opens at eight sharp, and it isn't eight, not yet. They can wait. For a precious few minutes, before the queue, Home Affairs belongs to me.

I am getting fat. I feel it when I squeeze through the narrow entrance that allows staff to go behind the counters. First, like I have done every day since taking on this job when the government changed in 1994, I fill the kettle.

"Ag nee, man." Someone has used my cup and left it, dirty, on the filing cabinet. They better not have eaten my chocolate digestives in the bottom drawer.

Miss Oliphant walks in just as the kettle boils.

"Mr Hendriks," she calls to me, "there is a nice little challenge waiting for you outside."

I hear her giggle.

"You can start with them, Miss Oliphant."

"No way, first come first served." She giggles again.

Miss Oliphant's slim frame is tucked into a colourful gypsy skirt and flimsy brown blouse. She teeters on gold high-heeled sandals that, she told me, she had bought the previous Saturday from a Nigerian with a blanket spread out at the taxi rank in town. They were some of the best shoes she had ever seen and her size four feet had slipped, like Cinderella's, easily into these glimmering towers.

Before Miss Oliphant works, she needs coffee. I know this and I wait at my desk for her to join me.

"Thanks for the best coffee in Oudtshoorn," she smiles and winks as she slides a small hand into my box of chocolate digestives.

I don't want to share my biscuits, but if I do I can watch a pretty ankle and gold-clad foot swing back and forth as she chews and sips for a few minutes.

After twenty minutes, when Miss Oliphant has eaten most of my biscuits and made herself more coffee, it is time to open up.

I look at the family through the window before I hook open the doors.

"Kom."

It takes them a few minutes to gather their things. They don't have much but the mother bosses them and they listen to her. The girl folds their only blanket and the boy carries a pot. The old man is a cripple with a stick but he has the toddler by the hand. They have tied a dog to the fence. The woman comes first, slowly, like she has all the time in the world.

"Kom mommy, kom, kom, kom," I say. "Wat soek julle?"

"Identities," they say in unison, even the children.

"Then you're in the right place." Miss Oliphant giggles behind me and I have to smile too.

I think the woman also smiles, but when I look at her again her eyes are down.

"We'll start with daddy, the rest of you sit over there."

There are rows of seats set well back where they can wait. Their smell is incredible. Strong enough to make a person cough. I am used to unwashed bodies, they face me every day, but this is different, this is straight out the veld. They smell of wood smoke and tobacco and sweat.

Miss Oliphant is covering her mouth and nose with her hand and giggling as she pretends to ignore me and work on her computer.

I have been trained to deal with people like this. It involves bend-ing rules and compromise, not something I am fond of doing, but nearly always inevitable with indigents.

"Right, daddy. Let's see what we can do about your identity. What is your name?"

For an identity you have to give the name your parents gave you, I explain. He can't be Kapok in his ID.

"My name is Joseph Bitterbessie," he says.

Name, enter, search. No point asking him to spell anything, he won't have a clue what I am talking about.

"Place of birth you say is Brakwater? What is the nearest town?" I tap-tap on the computer keys. "Ah, Leeu Gamka."

"Date of birth? You don't know? How old are you?"

The father has the body of an old man, bent double from hard labour, but his face is young. The skin is pinched around his eyes and his teeth are black stumps but his eyes still show some life. I estimate his date of birth as 1960.

"Who was your father, Mr Bitterbessie?"

"Ah yes."

There on the computer are the sketchy details of this itinerant's life. Someone, long ago, took the trouble to register him.

"You are lucky. The boer where your father worked when you were born had you registered."

It is unbelievable to find someone like this on the system. With any luck his woman and children will also prove easy. Today might just not be too bad. I fingerprint him and then, because I know I have to, I break all the rules and take the identity photos myself. No point in sending them all into town for that, they will never do it properly and my job is to ensure these people get ID books.

"Okay. You are done, you can sit. Mommy, kom."

Hopefully, someone long ago has registered this filthy creature too. Her parents are probably labourers. If they work for a good farmer she should be on the system. Some of the boere are meticulous about their staff's paperwork, others don't give a damn.

"Christina Muishond," is all she says.

Her eyes are filled with need and hope. If she isn't in the system it is going to be tricky. Who would have ever bothered with a nobody like this one? Her teeth are gone, just one or two on each side. She is tiny and her complexion is yellow, like her Boesman ancestors. The black rubber bangles on her wrists hang loose. A piece of animal skin is tied on one arm, to ward off evil. Her nose is small and hooked like a little witch and there is fight in her eyes. She has a stubborn mouth.

"Where did you people walk from?" I ask, genuinely interested.

"Leeu Gamka, Meneer." She lowers her face when she sees me studying her.

"Why didn't you wait for the Home Affairs truck to come there?"

"We are never there on the same day as the truck," she says simply.

"So, you trek to Oudtshoorn?"

She is not in the system. This one is going to take some doing.

"Where did you grow up?"

"Gansvlei, Meneer."

"Nee man, what was the nearest big town?"

She thinks for a moment.

"Fraserburg, Meneer."

"How old are you?" She shakes her head.

To get her on the system I need to fill in an E55. There is one in the filing cabinet at the back of the office. Slowly, painstakingly, I begin outlining the details of this pathetic creature's existence. She doesn't have all the answers. Sometimes the father limps forward to see if he can provide a detail. But she knows the basics: her name, her parents' names and where she was born. Dates are a blank. She has no concept of years or days or months and I look hard at her before estimating her age at thirty-seven. A hard life might make this too high. I give her my late mother's birthday, 26 January. The year of her birth I write as 1974.

After an hour, when I can see she is battling to concentrate, I say she can sit down. I am going to take a break, then we can start on the children.

"Mr Hendriks, why don't you eat your polony sandwich?" Miss Oliphant says kindly, unwrapping it for me and putting it next to my mug. I go into the office at the back, switch the kettle on again and, for a little while, I close my eyes.

None of the children have been registered but there are procedures to deal with that. When I ask about the boy's father a flicker of concern crosses the mother's face and I know instantly the father isn't the boy's biological parent.

"Who is his father?"

"He is dead," she says.

The production of a death certificate and an affidavit should be the procedure, but naturally there is little chance of that ever happening.

"Breaking all the rules today, are we?" Miss Oliphant whispers. She knows she will never be allowed to do what I am doing.

"We will register him without a father," I decide.

They are at my mercy and today I am being merciful.

The little girls are easy. The man nods enthusiastically when asked if they are his. The beauty of our system is that birth certificates are instant and I am able to give this mangy little group something immediately. The printer at the back of the room purrs. One by one each of the children's birth certificates tick-tick out of the machine and I lay them carefully on the counter.

Johannus Stephanus Muishond.

Charmaine Eloise Muishond.

Elisma Magrieta Muishond.

Beautiful, careful names given to each child by their mother. It makes me a little tearful thinking about it. They aren't married so I give them their mother's surname. Fathers seldom stay, mothers never leave.

"This one is for your son, this is for your big girl and this one is for your baby."

"Dankie, Meneer."

I fold them and push them into a brown envelope.

This might give them an extra few months of life. I won't bother with birth certificates for the adults. Identity books are enough.

"Pas hulle op, dis amptelike dokumente," I say with a stern face.

For the first time the woman's eyes meet mine and she smiles. The desperation is gone and in its place is joy. She nods.

"Your IDs will be ready in four months. You must come back. September, nè? Do you understand when September is?"

"It is when the veld flowers bloom, that is when we will come back," she says.

"Yes, when the flowers are in bloom, then you come back, you hear me?"

She wraps the envelope in a doek and pushes it to the bottom of the plastic bag carrying her few things. I can only imagine what those papers will look like by the time these kids reach eighteen.

Miss Oliphant chuckles and whispers, "Mr Hendriks, at least they are in the system."

The family walks out into the morning sunshine and stands for a few minutes under the tree. The mother and father share a rolled cigarette.

Inside, the queue is long and I summon a chubby pink woman who demands to know when her passport will be ready as she is leaving for her holiday in Europe in a week.

I walk to the filing cabinet to look for it and say a prayer of thanks when I find it. This is one of those rare days when I am actually making people happy.

I look out the window to see the family again, but they are gone.

42 MUIS

The paper is stiff and smells like Jik. Each letter of each name is black on yellow paper.

The letters mean names but I can't understand them. "J", like Jan, is Fansie's name, Johannus Stephanus, the name of his father and the name of my father together. I follow the line with my finger. These papers are my children's lives. They have faces because the government has written down their names on these papers and made them into people.

"Yes, the clinic can see your baby because she has a birth certificate."

"Yes, the girl can come to school, thank you for the birth certificate."

"Yes, you can have All Pay because your child exists."

"Keep these papers safe, mommy," the big fat man at Home Affairs says. I want to say, "These are my children's lives, I will carry them next to my heart."

He folds them and puts them in a brown envelope. When we are outside, I take the brown envelope in my packet and tie it with string and tuck it inside my shirt.

We don't go back to the river. After Home Affairs we walk to town because we have the money from Miskiet's pockets and Kapok says we need supplies. We look for a shop where we can buy a hamper but there are so many shops and so many cars that we don't know where to go. It is hard, with people bumping into us and cars hooting. Witpop is walking like she is in a dream and I shout at Fansie to hold her hand or she will get lost or knocked over. When we can't find the right shop Kapok asks a man and he tells us to go to the Chinese.

"They've got a hamper shop," the man says. "Rows and rows of hampers."

Ja, that's what we want.

"Where?"

"One block down, this side," he shows us with his hands and we understand.

When we walk on again, Kapok whispers to me, "He also can't read, like us."

I nod. The man doesn't say, "Left, then right and left again," because then we will never find our way.

We find the shop and choose a hamper for R200 with flour, sugar and coffee. Sponsie is so excited because when we open it there is a bottle of green cooldrink too. It is a good hamper. There are also four tins of fish, curry powder, fish oil, lemon creams and a packet of candles. The woman at the till is Chinese. I have never seen a Chinese before and, while we are looking through the hampers, I peep at her face. It is interesting to see a white that is so different. She doesn't look like a Boer. When we pay she takes our money without smiling and gives us change, then sits down on her chair again and stares out the window like before. Her mind is far away, I think, visiting a place where I will never go.

We walk slowly up the main street of Oudtshoorn. People rush past us, shouting to their friends on the other side of the street. Fruit sellers sit on the pavement holding up packets of bananas.

"Come my lady, nice bananas my lady, R5, R5."

Clothes hang in the windows of shops, shoes, chairs, bicycles: all these things to buy with money. Kapok is sniffing the air like a dog.

"What's it?"

I sniff too and then it hits me and my stomach squeezes. It is a smell like no other and my mouth begins to water. The pavement where we are standing, sniffing, is busy. Men are loading boxes on to a truck and we need to move out the way.

"It's inside," one of them shouts at Kapok.

"Go and buy that skinny chick some food so she can stop drooling." They all laugh and I stare at them. Fat men with greasy shirts and rolls of stomach hanging over their pants.

Before I can say anything Kapok goes inside. Behind a glass counter are pieces of fried fish, chicken and chips and shining red Russians.

The lady looks at him with a packet in her hands, ready to fill.

"Two Russians and a big chips," he says, "and a two-litre Coke."

Behind me Fansie starts laughing when he realises what his pappie is doing and Sponsie claps her hands. Witpop looks at me, her eyes still empty.

The lady smiles at the children as she heaps our food on a sheet of white paper.

"Salt and vinegar?"

She speaks too fast for Kapok to understand, so he just nods. With one hand she shakes salt and with the other she splatters brown vinegar over everything, then she folds the paper over and rolls the hot food into a parcel and hands it to Kapok. He gives her one of Miskiet's notes and she scratches in her money box for change.

"Dankie, Mevrou," he says. We walk outside, all of us not believing what has happened. The corner outside the shop is too busy for us to eat there, so we cross the road, walking on for a while to a low wall, near some men who are smoking.

Witpop hasn't talked since she shot Miskiet and now I take her by the shoulders and say, "Wake up, Witpop, we are going to have Russians and chips, wake up." She nods but her eyes are dead and I feel a sadness in my heart.

"You must eat because we have a long walk to get back over the mountains."

Kapok breaks the sausages in half and takes tiny pieces of his own and gives it to Sponsie and Rinkhals. Then he divides the chips into four heaps and each of us eat, enjoying the sharp taste of the vinegar and the grease of the sausage. Sponsie eats a handful of chips and her sausage then she rests her little head on my chest, closes her eyes and sleeps.

"That's the sleep of a full stomach," says Kapok, his lips shining from the food.

Kapok wipes his hands on his pants then digs into his shirt pocket for his little orange bag of tobacco. He rolls a skuif from a piece of the chip paper and lights it. After he has drawn in the smoke he hands it to me and he walks over to the men for a chat. They are guarding the whites' cars, they say. The people give them a R2 when they come back from shopping.

"Who are you guarding it from?"

"Mafelletjies." Street children.

Kapok nods. Mafelletjies would steal from a car. I think about a time once in Prince Albert when they stole our donkeys in the middle of the night. When the police came to call us they were running in the main street and we had to go fetch them. It took us a long time to tame the animals after that and Pantoffel had a scar on her face where she had been hit with a brick. It would have been worth it to pay someone a R2 to guard them.

Lucky for them there are no mafelletjies today and the men don't have to chase anyone.

"This is a lazy way to make money, smoking and talking and then wanting a R2 just for being here," Kapok tells the oompie. "Jirre, you must work on Baas Jannie's farm. There a man has to shear four sheep for a R2."

"It's good money here," the oompie says to Kapok. "But hey, this is my place. You can't come guard here or else it is trouble for you." We all laugh when he says that, we are in a good mood now, with full stomachs.

"Nee, oompie," Kapok says, "we don't want to guard cars. We are going back over the mountain to our place in the Great Karoo."

"Man, that's far," the oompie says.

We will walk over the mountains because we don't have the donkey cart.

"The road we are taking now is not easy with donkeys," Kapok says to the man. "This road is called the Swartberg Pass."

The oompie knows about the Swartberg Pass. "That's a long way to walk," he says.

"Yes, they say at Die Top you can see all the way to Fraserburg. That's where my wife was born."

I didn't know you could see all the way to Fraserburg and I wonder if I would be able to see my mother's house on the farm.

We fall asleep in the sun and, when I open my eyes, Kapok and Fansie are gone. Witpop's head is resting on my shoulder and she is snoring softly. I don't move but watch the oompie parking cars and collecting his R2s.

When he sees I am awake he says Kapok will come back soon.

"Hy het net vir hom 'n ietsie gaan koop." He laughs. Kapok is chasing a dop.

I feel the packet inside my shirt. My children's identities are safe and they are sleeping because they have eaten. So I rest, with Sponsie on my chest and Witpop at my side.

43   FANSIE

Pappie wants a dop. I know it straight away when I look at his face. That hardegat secret thing is in his eyes, like when he has made up his mind and there is no stopping him.

Mamma is sleeping sitting up straight, with Sponsie on her lap and Witpop leaning against her. I have been sitting warm in the sun, half watching the oompie park cars and half dreaming about taking a dronkie's money. Witpop has Rinkhals tied to her ankle with a string.

"Fansie, I am going to take a look around," Pappie says. "You stay here."

When he gets up, so do I.

"Stay here."

I don't say anything but walk after him and he stops and looks at me and makes like he will klap me, but I laugh. When he is looking for a dop he doesn't fight with me. He shrugs and walks on. The oompie has told him where the bottle store is and now shouts after him, "Hey ou pel, bring vir my ook 'n doppie, man!"

Pappie doesn't look back. He heads down the road the way the oompie showed him, not caring if I am coming or staying. He is like this when he is chasing a dop. A truck could run us all over and he will just carry on walking to find his wyntjie.

The bottle store is next to a big warehouse that has bakkies loaded with tin cans and sacks of frozen chicken coming and going all the time. It is nice to watch the men throw the packs of cans to each other and stack them. They load bakkies quickly and I see a Ramadaan from the lokasie shop in Prince Albert pointing and arguing with the guys and making them change everything on the back. When he leaves, his bakkie is so loaded it looks like it is scraping on the ground.

Pappie takes a pink note from the money we took off the dead oom and holds it between his thumb and a finger so the people in the bottle store will know he means business and he isn't in there to steal. Sometimes, when we are in bottle stores without money, for Pappie to enjoy the smell, the security guard will follow us and then take Pappie by the elbows and push him out. At times like that Pappie goes nearly mad from the smell of the dop. Tears chase each other down his cheeks, but there is nothing he can do. The feeling passes after a while but his body cries; it is so thirsty for a wyntjie.

Today he has money and he takes his time, walking up and down looking at the bottles. I stay at the front watching him.

At last he finds what he wants, a big plastic bottle of wine that looks like pee.

He puts it on the till and a white woman takes the R50 and gives him a slip. No change. For a moment Pappie waits then she says, "Dis dit!" He picks up the wine and comes outside.

"Whew, that's a big one, Pappie." He looks pleased and I know he can't wait to have a slukkie.

"Go fetch Mamma and your sisters and I will wait here."

"Are you going to get drunk here?"

It is a dangerous place to dop, the lady in the bottle store is watching us and a police car will be here soon if we open the bottle.

"There is a parkie a little way up this road. I'll go dop in a corner there. You know where it is?"

"Come back with me, Pappie."

"Nee, that oompie will want my wine."

"Give me a slukkie?"

"Not here, come walk up the road."

When we are a little way up the road near the park Pappie loosens the white cap and hands me the bottle. It is heavy but I hold it like a man and take a long sluk.

"Hey, hey, don't drink it all." He grabs the bottle back and a little splashes on the pavement. The wine burns in my throat, but I smile a big smile and Pappie laughs. It makes me want to vomit and I hold on to a wooden fence, worrying that the Russian and chips are going to come out when I really want them to stay in.

Behind the fence, dogs are barking. Pappie laughs again and I shake my head and then walk slowly up the road thinking that wine really does make a person feel dof.

The oompie is collecting money from a white woman who can't find a R2. He is standing waiting, watching her while she digs in her bag. I think he is hoping she will drop paper money and then he will slide his foot over it while she carries on looking for a coin.

Mamma is awake and when she sees me she stands up. Witpop is awake too and we pick up our bags and slip away without saying goodbye to the old man.

I take them to the park where Pappie is waiting and Witpop lies down again with Sponsie and Rinkhals in the plants and they go back to sleep.

Pappie and Mamma start drinking and I watch them. First it is that thirsty drinking when they gulp the wine, spilling it and snatching it from each other. After a while Mamma's eyes stare at the ground and her bottom lip hangs loose. She tries to stand up but just lands up sitting down again. Pappie curls up next to Witpop and Sponsie with the bottle in his arms and falls asleep. Slowly Mamma lies down too and her eyes close. The night is coming and it is cool. I rub my arms to keep warm. We have no fire because we don't want the whites to see us sleeping in their parkie, using their plants for a soft bed. I watch them for a long time. Sponsie's baby face is so peaceful, her tiny arms are up above her head. The sore at the corner of Witpop's mouth is crusty and yellow. She sucks her thumb and I watch her mouth move in her sleep. Pappie is snoring, his legs wide open, a dronkie sleeping who doesn't care what can happen to him, like mafelletjies putting their hands in his pockets and stealing all his money. Like me. Mamma's hands are under her cheek and her face is still. Her worn-out shoes are lying in the bushes nearby. Rinkhals looks at me then puts his head down and sleeps.

Pappie wants to walk over the mountains tomorrow. Too many people have seen us, he says. We need to slip away and disappear on the plains. I think about the vlaktes. The koppies shining in the heat. The sound of a windmill pumping out hidden water from the ground. A little duikertjie watching me from its rocky ridge.

I am hungry again and I stand up and walk to the bottom of the road and look up at the Swartberg that we have to cross. Tonight the mountains are far away and very high.

I carry on walking, thinking I will go back to that lokasie where I stole the bread yesterday.

When I get to the Kentucky in the main street there are boys, like me, sitting against the wall. One of them is working the cars driving up to fetch food. He is trying to score a piece of chicken but most people are chasing him and giving him nothing.

A little one with cheeky eyes sees me and shouts, "Hey, wie's jy?"

"Nee, wie's jy?" I answer. I know boys like this. They will have knives. But so do I. Both the oom's knives are in my pockets and I push my hand in and let my fingers close around one.

The boy laughs. "Boetie! Ek is Boetie."

"Wie se boetie?"

"Vetkoek se boetie and he is in jail for murder." He makes his eyes wide when he says this but I can see he is joking and I laugh.

"Ek is Fansie." *And I also know about murder.*

"I have seen you before," says Boetie, "in Prince Albert."

"You know Prince Albert?" I am surprised.

"My father once worked for Meneer Danie in the Weltevrede."

I know of Meneer Danie.

"Shearing?"

"No, fences and watermelons."

"My pappie did shearing for Meneer Clive. Goats."

"Ja, I know Meneer Clive."

We are friends now. The other boys are bigger but he is their leader. They are called Klonkie, Kokkerot and Joburg.

"Come sit with us," says Boetie. I can't help it but I feel a big smile coming on my face.

That night we don't sleep. We talk and laugh and I share a skuif with them. When the Kentucky closes, one of the women gives us each a piece of chicken and some burnt chips and we walk off to an empty piece of ground where the other boys sleep and Boetie and I talk.

When the sun rises we head towards the lokasie to look for more food. It is only much later that I remember Pappie and Mamma and my sisters. I wonder if they have started walking. I look at the black mountains but then Boetie calls. The boys have found a dronkie and he has money.

44 MUIS

All day we walk towards the mountains. Kapok says this is a short cut so that we don't have to go back through Meiringspoort. I wouldn't mind going back the same way but he is afraid he will see Pantoffel and Rinnik and that will mean too much pain. The road to the Swartberg Pass from Oudtshoorn is long but quiet with good places to rest. There is so much water. Much more than on the other side of the mountains, where there is nothing. When night comes we settle under high blue gums next to the river. The river is clean and there are plenty of stokkies for a fire. We eat a tin of pilchards and a packet of lemon creams from the hamper with sweet coffee. Without Miskiet looking for us I am at peace and, for the first time in many, many years, sleep comes easily with the night. The cold wakes me in the early hours and I lie for a long time watching the stars through the still branches of the trees and listening to the crickets. We will need all our blankets soon – they are in Rietbron with Diksop. We can fetch them when we are over the mountains.

The moon is big and I can see the river so I stand up and walk along the bank, picking up sticks. The bright eyes of a muishond freeze as it watches me come.

"Dis okay muishond, ek is ook 'n muishond."

Miskiet is dead, I live.

"Ek is 'n muishond," I say aloud, the only sound in the dead night. The animal runs into the bushes and is gone.

I will not hide anymore.

When we fetch our blankets we will go back to Prince Albert. I will get a domestic job and the children will go to school. We will rent a space in a yard and make a proper hok. Kapok must find sinkplaat so we can build a hok. In the morning, when we walk over the Swartberg, I will tell him my plans.

At the camp I make a small fire for coffee and then lie next to the red coals with my cup.

Witpop is awake and in a thin, sleepy voice she asks me, "Mamma, why are you laughing?"

I stretch out and touch her head. It is good to hear her talking again.

"I didn't laugh."

"I heard you laugh, Mamma."

"A big rock that I have carried on my shoulders is gone."

"Was the rock the oom?"

"Ja. It was the oom. He wanted to kill me because I wouldn't do what he wanted."

"'n Man kannie so maak'ie, Mamma."

For a while we lie, listening to the river.

"I shot him, Mamma."

Kapok is sitting up now too, rubbing his eyes and looking at the fire. I add more sticks and push the coffee-pot into the coals again.

"Is there any of Miskiet's money left?" I ask him.

"R200."

"Give me R150. I want to keep it safe so that when we are over these high mountains I can take Witpop to Pep and buy her school shoes and roll-on."

Witpop is staring into the fire but when I say that she lifts her face to me and I see her tired, dead eyes become alive again.

"Dankie," I say to her. "Dankie, my kind," and, for the first time since she fired that gun, she smiles.

The next morning we reach the mountains and our climb starts. The Swartberg Pass is a road that twists and turns into the clouds.

As we walk I look back to see if Fansie is coming but there is no one.

Kapok walks in front and every time he stops for a rest he climbs on a rock to look back over the way we have come.

At last, at Die Top, we can see the plains of the Great Karoo on the other side. Kapok says Fraserburg is out there but I can't see it. It isn't true, a person can't see all that way. I don't know why I believed Kapok when he said that. He was talking rubbish.

"Climb up to the peak, you will see it from there," he says.

"I have just climbed a mountain and now you want me to climb more so I can see a town? Is jy mal?"

He just laughs and I smile at him. "I want to sit now," I say.

We make camp off the road, in a small hollow out of the wind. Tonight, on top of this mountain, it is going to be cold. We sit close together, laughing at Sponsie's chattering. Kapok kills the fire as soon as our coffee boils and the tin of beans is hot.

"This is not a place for fires, people will chase us," he says.

Then, when the dark comes, I see the lights, far-away stars at the end of the sky. "That's the Ultra City at Leeu Gamka," Kapok says.

"That is very far away," I say, thinking how long it took us to get to the mountains.

"Do you want to go there again?" he asks.

"If there is no work this side, we can go there and send word for Baas Kobus and Klein Mies that we have come."

Miskiet is gone. Leeu Gamka is our place too, and we can go back.

The lights are all that shows there is a town. From Die Top I can't see there is a road with trucks going to Cape Town or houses with people. There is a tunnel there, a place where one thing changed everything.

"We haven't got money for more donkeys," Kapok says. He is thinking aloud. "It's too hard now with donkeys and only the langkampe for grazing and then nothing in drought times. I am glad we don't have donkeys anymore. I couldn't stand their hungry eyes for another day," he says.

I understand. It is hard with a karretjie now.

The packet with my children's papers is close to my heart and I reach into my shirt and touch it. The government knows their names and their faces. Miskiet said Fansie was his child but this is not so.

Miskiet wanted a woman and a child and I feel sorry for him, even though, all this time, I was afraid of him.

Kapok is watching me and he says, "A person can't own another person. Everyone is free and karretjiemense are more free than any-one. God made it like that."

It's true. Miskiet would have been a hard man to live with. I would have been like Aunty Loos, hit on the head so many times they would have had to put me in the ground. There would have been no one for my children then. It is better this way.

Jan, who died in the tunnel so long ago, never knew he would have been a father. He never touched a dop and I think, if he had been alive, maybe I would have been a dorpsvrou.

Ja, Kapok makes me walk up and down, this way and that way, but it is okay. There are many happy times.

Under the sky, on the quiet mountain, I think about where Fansie is sleeping. Many times he sleeps alone in the veld but towns are not good places for him.

"Mamma, Fansie will find us," Witpop says. "He knows the road we are taking. He will come."

"Yes, Witpop," I say, "he will find us." I smile at her. My Witpop.

He will come.

He always does.